To Nicole Iaione,

Enjoy!

signature

9-18-21

Veronica

by RJ Bonett

Cover design by: Ronald Bonett
Grateful appreciation to: Charlene Lewis for content approval.

Kandace Rollman Wortz: Editor
Karen DeLise: Photography and assistance for front cover.

Photo Restoration
New York Camera & Video
1139 Street Road
Southampton, Pa. 18966

Introduction

A quiet walk along the water's edge at the beach after a storm- can at times act as a cleansing agent to Ron Bennett, a freelance reporter for the *Evening Bulletin*, a Philadelphia newspaper. His stories at times are mired in tragedy and corruption that make this 60 mile trip from the city a necessity. The discovery of a human arm protruding from a sand dune on Long Beach Island, New Jersey, will alter his life. Seeking a telephone to summon authorities, he meets Veronica, a woman standing on the walkway looking out at the ocean. His opinion of her extravagant beach front home, encroaching on his quiet place is one of the changes on the island he didn't care for. The chance meeting on several trips to the shore begins an interest in a relationship he desires, and believes the feelings are mutual. The innuendos about an abusive husband Joel- create a stronger desire to get her to come to her senses and leave him. After seeing marks on her neck as if she was being strangled, his frustration becomes a compulsive effort to convince her every time they meet to leave her husband. He gets caught up in a situation that would make the worst story he covered, pale by comparison.

Chapter 1

There's something special about walking the beach after a storm. The surf churns up seashells and other odd objects, like old bottles and driftwood. A person has the best chance of making a rare find early in the morning, before anyone else gets there. It was that sort of day in late September 1975, as I walked the water's edge on Long Beach Island in New Jersey. The sky was a beautiful blue, with pure white billowing clouds. The crisp, cool air was coming inland, typical weather after a hurricane or major storm. Gulls were taking advantage of the breeze, soaring with open wings and letting the wind keep them aloft. Occasionally, one would spy a piece of fish washed up on shore, and it would be a race to the prize, each one trying to outmaneuver the other.

The new school year had begun a few weeks earlier. Families that vacation on the island had already abandoned it to return to their primary homes and routines for another 9 or 10 months.

They would have only the memories of the past summer to carry them through the long winter, until next year's vacation. The older people, who generally inhabit the island this time of year to avoid the younger crowds, were chased out by the hurricane that was predicted, but didn't quite live up to expectations.

I always liked Beach Haven, a community on the south end of Long Beach Island. The island is nothing more than a sand bar- a barrier island, 15 miles long and a half- mile wide. It's nature's natural barrier to protect the mainland and estuaries for small fishes and other aquatic marine life to begin their life cycle. It's something that was never meant to be built on.

The island is divided into seven townships from Barnegat Light House on the north end- to Beach Haven on the south end. In almost every township along the main corridor, some Victorian homes still exist, landmarks of the original islanders. They were testimony of a bygone era, written in stone and wood, when a 20 minute ferry ride across the bay from the mainland, wasn't an inconvenience. The tranquility and an occasional stroll along the ocean were probable well worth the effort.

Later, people would bravely traverse a rickety wooden planked bridge that had to be closed whenever a severe storm threatened. In its waning years, the planks that supported the traffic would make a sound as though they were loose- raising an alarm that made you wonder whether you were going to make the distant shore.

In 1954, Hurricane Hazel ended the life of the old bridge, and a four lane concrete bridge replaced it.

Those who planned the new bridge had the foresight to make it two lanes in each direction, although the roads before and after the bridge were still one lane each way. Obviously, they had foreseen the expansion that was to come. A few people were bold enough to defy the devastation of Hurricane Hazel, but were still cautious about such an investment. Others seeing them were emboldened by their pioneering spirit. It also helped a great deal when the Federal Flood Insurance Program came into existence. No longer would people be on their own, taking a chance on losing everything due to a storm. Uncle Sam was there to help.

What started out as a trickle of land purchases and a few homes being built soon resembled the land rush in Oklahoma. People flocked to the island on weekends, armed with a few tools and friends or relatives who helped them build their homes. With more houses cropping up every year, a new era of development began. For $1,800 two bedroom pre-fabricated Sears Roebuck Homes, sprang up. They were delivered to your lot, complete with instructions, ready for assembly. It became a weekend pass time for people from as far away as New York City and Philadelphia, as well as the surrounding area.

In the last 15 years or so, the small two bedroom homes that were beachfront were being bought, not for their value, but the value of the land they occupied, and in most instances, were torn down. The large homes constructed on those sites were built as a testimony to wealth. Towering three- story structures with rooftop decks- were visible from party boats, several miles offshore. Elaborate to the point of being ridiculous, they blocked the view of the homes further inland.

I didn't care for the change and always thought the smaller homes as weekend retreats. I wondered why anyone would want to come here for a restful weekend, and have to worry about maintaining a second home instead of fishing or just relaxing. It sort of defeats its original purpose. I guess that's why I enjoyed Beach Haven more than any other part of the island. It was at the extreme end, and development was just beginning to get seriously underway. It still had Victorians and was less crowded even during the season, being distant from the family type motels and amusement centers.

After I crossed the causeway bridge, I made my right onto the main road heading south toward Beach Haven. Almost at my destination, I noticed some demolition activity close to where I usually park. Two more homes were being demolished and a large 4- by- 8 sign, was prominently displayed on the corner of the property: "Coming soon. To be erected on this site, a 4,200 square foot home." The name of the contractor was at the bottom of the sign: Carl Dunn Inc., General Contractor and Builder. I looked almost with reverence at the homes being destroyed. This was something I didn't like seeing- but hey, that's "progress."

After I pulled into a parking spot several blocks away, I reached into the rear seat and got my dog Daisy's leash. We crossed the walkway over the sand dunes and went down to the beach.

Daisy's a great dog and has been my constant companion coming to the beach with me for the five years I've had her. Upon reaching the beach, she would sit patiently until I unhooked her leash, setting her free- and with a burst of energy- she would run to the water's edge. The energy she released was as if she had received a shot of adrenalin. The liberation from being cooped up in an apartment most of the week, with only a twice daily walk for her constitutional, was well appreciated.

I was particularly enjoying the beach that day, walking along the shoreline. I had just finished a corruption story for the *Evening Bulletin,* a newspaper in Philadelphia. Dealing with different people and stories sometimes mired with tragedy or corruption wasn't easy. It's not like doing social reporting, or outright news stories; mine as we say, can get down and dirty.

For me, a trip to the shore is a cleansing treatment- like a shower after a hard day's work and at times much needed. What people wouldn't do for the almighty dollar never ceased to amaze me.

Unlike Daisy who braved the waves, I would retreat up the beach every time a wave came in a little closer. Daisy occasionally would put her snout close to the water, getting some of it up her nose, then would pull back and sneeze. She always ran ahead chasing seagulls that were always a step ahead of her. Sometimes they would wait until she became an immediate threat- not completely taking flight, but flapping their wings and moving another five yards away. It seemed as though they were playing a game, and Daisy would either tire or find something else to attract her attention.

I lived in Philadelphia, 65 miles away, and the commute was no problem, especially given the prospect of a nice day at the ocean. I would come down to the island as often as I could during the year, to either go out on charter boats or surf fish from one of the rock jetties. The jetties are for the purpose of keeping this fragile strip of land intact; fishing from them is a side benefit. I've found that the best time of year to jetty fish is in the fall, when migratory fish are heading south, and the bait fish are more abundant and closer to shore.

Successful fishing from the surf or jetties requires a little knowledge of the action of the water around the rock structures- and holes under the water- caused by waves and tidal action. This can differ with each of the 50 or more jetties that extend from different points on the island. I brought my surf gear today, and even if I didn't use it because the surf was still very sandy from the storm, I had been eager to get out of the city for awhile.

Often while walking the beach with Daisy, I'd encounter other people walking their dogs, and I'd stop and chat with someone. Most of the time our conversation would start with commenting about our dogs, and anyone who has ever owned one knows their social attributes. Daisy's a unique dog with her markings- all white with the exception of five small brown spots on her left ear, and a distinct brown shaped heart over part of her face. Her hunting instincts come from her breeding which includes Labrador retriever, part hound and part pointer. When she sees something of interest, her front leg raises and her thick tail sticks straight out. She's a perfect match for me, and a great comfort and companion.

If people would get the message dogs convey, life would be so much easier. As the saying goes, "Dogs wag their tails instead of their tongues." They're generally friendly, until they get a threatening response.

We hadn't seen anyone else today, but Daisy was drawn to a stretch of sand dunes where there were no houses. I wondered what she was doing sniffing around and thought she may have discovered a dead seagull. I called her to *"come!"_*which she would always do without hesitation, but she was fixated on something behind the sand dune. She stayed there looking at me, wagging her tail to let me know it wasn't an act of defiance, but something she wanted me to see.

As I approached her, I looked over the first dune and saw what I thought might have been the left hand and forearm of a mannequin sticking out of the sand. On closer examination, I realized it wasn't a mannequin but a human hand with a ring still on the third finger. It didn't appear to have any signs of decomposition, and I chose not to disturb whatever evidence that might be surrounding it. At this point, I didn't know whether it was only an arm and hand, or whether there was a body attached. I stuck a piece of drift wood I found in the sand as a marker and put a leash on Daisy. I had to walk about a 100 yards to get back to the wooden walkway that led over the sand dunes. As I began to walk up the steps, there was a woman standing at the top staring at the sea. She was wearing a peach colored sheer wrap around that was blowing gently in the breeze. With her high cheek bones and her slim neck line, she looked almost goddess- like.

With her pose she could have easily been a model for a beautiful wood carving that adorned the bow of the most regal wooden ship__ a true goddess. She was well built and appeared to be in her late 30's. She had below- the- shoulder length brown hair that had a reddish tint in the morning sunlight.

"Good morning."

Looking at me, she smiled to acknowledge my greeting, but didn't say anything.

"Do you live nearby? I have to make a phone call."

"Is it an emergency?"

"My dog Daisy found a human arm sticking out of a sand dune, about a hundred yards down the beach."

Her facial expression immediately turned from inquisitive- to surprisingly shocked, trying to absorb what I told her. After a few moments fumbling for the right words... "You're kidding me –right?"

"I know it's not exactly what you usually hear after giving someone a good morning greeting, but no, I'm very serious."

She was obviously unnerved at my comment but pointed to the second house from the walkway. "That's where I live." She said starting off in that direction. "You can use my phone. Is it a man's hand or a woman's?"

"It looks like a woman's. There's what appears to be a woman's ring on her finger."

I followed her to one of the newer, more modern homes built within the last few years.

"Your house is beautiful." But in the back of my mind, it was one of the changes I really didn't care for. "It must be great to sit out on your deck and watch the ocean whenever you want?"

"It is. My husband Joel and I had it built three years ago by a local builder, Carl Dunn. Do you know him?"

"No, not personally, but I see his signs on quite a few job sites where houses are being built on the island."

I looked around... "Looks like he's pretty successful- He did a great job on your home."

"He's very talented, a really good builder. He's probably the fore-most contractor and developer for most of the new homes going up in Beach Haven- for that matter probably on Long Beach Island. He and his wife Carla became very good friends of my husband Joel and I when he was building the house."

After reaching her patio, I looked around for a place to attach Daisy's chain. "Would you mind if I wrap this around the arm of this deck chair? I don't want to bring her inside. She has a lot of sand on her."

"That's fine. Come in, the phone's is in the kitchen."

After securing Daisy's chain, I made sure I wiped the sand from my shoes first before stepping inside. Looking at the kitchen was like looking at a page in Better Homes and Gardens magazine. It had every modern convenience, right down to the cherry wood cabinets and green marble counter tops- a real beauty.

"Have a seat. I'll get the phone number for you."

As she handed me the refrigerator magnet with emergency phone numbers, she introduced herself. "By the way, my name's Veronica-Veronica Simmons. And you are?"

"I'm sorry my name's Ron Bennett."

Then I turned my attention back to the pad dialing the first num-ber, which was the police. She told me her address, and I relayed it to the person I was speaking to.

"Would you like a cup of coffee since you have to wait for the patrol car? It's kind of chilly this morning."

"Yes, the air is a little chilly. Coffee sounds great."

Sitting at the kitchen table, I couldn't help but notice the size of her wedding ring as she poured my coffee. It was as big as a jellybean. That, plus the furnishings in the house and the house itself, I surmised her and her husband were wealthy. Looking out into the spacious living room, the walls were a light mint green color, with light gray carpeting. The L- shaped sofa and chair were white with chrome and glass end tables flanking them. Peach- colored ceramic lamps were on both tables with white shades- perfect pastel colors for a sea shore home. On one wall was a green stone fireplace, and in the corner was a modern floor standing vase with long metallic stems and large tropical leaves. Modern abstract art hung on two walls, and two masks of Comedy and Tragedy were carefully spaced over the fireplace. A spiral staircase rose from what looked like a wide hall at the far end of the room that led to the upstairs. A real beauty- and I wondered what the rest of the house looked like.

"Veronica, are you a full time resident?"

"No, I live just outside Philadelphia. I come down a lot during the off season. I enjoy coming down in the spring and fall when the weather isn't so warm, and the island's less crowded."

Taking the pot from the counter, she began emptying it into a coffee carafe, spilling some. When she got to the table, I could see her hands were trembling, still nervous about Daisy's find.

"You still look a little shaky. I better pour the coffee before you spill it."

"Thanks, I am. This thing has me completely unnerved this morning. Would you like a pastry with your coffee? I have some fresh from the bakery."

"No thanks, just coffee will be fine."

"Do you think the hand and arm are part of a complete body?"

"I don't know. I didn't want to disturb anymore than I had to until the police have a chance to do their work."

"Could it have been someone who drowned during the hurricane and washed ashore- The sea level did get that high."

"I know. I saw the high water mark on the dunes, but I really can't say. In any case, I don't think the tidal action would have buried her that deep if it is a complete body."

I only had a chance to take a few sips of coffee when the patrol car arrived. I went outside and unchained Daisy as the officer got out of his car.

"I'm Policeman Benjamin Davis, Beach Haven Police Department. Did you call?"

If you close your eyes and had to envision a typical small town policeman-, it would probably resemble Officer Davis. He was a tall, muscular man. I'd say around my age- in his early 40's, with a tinge of gray, mixed in with his black hair.

"I'm Ron Bennett, as I extended my hand. My dog found a hand and forearm sticking out of a sand dune, about a hundred yards down the beach."

I pointed in that direction. He looked toward the section of beach I was referring to then reached for his cap.

"Would you show me where it is?"

"I'll be glad to, officer."

"Good morning, Ma'am."

"I'm sorry, officer. This is Veronica- Veronica Simmons. This is her house. She let me use her phone."

"Carl Dunn was the builder who did this house, wasn't he Ma'am?"

"Yes officer. Do you know him?"

"Carl and I went to school together. We're both islanders."

Escorting the officer to the walkway, I turned to Veronica. "Thanks for the use of the phone and the coffee, Mrs. Simmons."

"No problem. Please, call me Veronica. If you find out who the person is could you let me know?"

"I'll come back and tell you everything I find out."

I walked down the beach with Officer Davis, relating my story of how Daisy and I discovered the hand. When we reached the marker, I pointed to it. Going over the sand dune, he knelt down next to it, slowly moving a little sand to see how far down the arm extended, and uncovered it up to the arm pit. A little more loose sand fell away, and I could see part of the torso.

"Officer, is it a complete body?"

"I don't know yet. It appears it might be. I don't want to disturb anything that may help with an investigation."

He continued carefully moving more sand, and in a few minutes, more of the upper body was exposed.

"Yes, I think this is a whole body, I better call the station, I'll need more help to uncover this. We don't have the ability to do forensic work- we rely on the state police. It's something we don't have in a small township. Would you mind staying until I return, I won't be gone long, probably about 20 minutes. I want to get a camera and a few evidence bags."

"No problem. Do whatever you have to do."

Ten minutes after he walked away, Veronica came down the beach and stopped where I was standing.

"Ron, is it a full body, a real human?"

"I'm afraid so. The rest of the body is still buried. The officer went to get more equipment to uncover it. He said he has to call the state police to help with the investigation. I volunteered to wait until he gets back with more help. I imagine it will take a little while for them to return. Did your curiosity of wanting to see the body get the best of you?"

"No, it's something I don't need to see. When I saw the officer leave, I thought you may have been wrong about it being a human. Now that you've told me it's real, I'd like to see whether I know the person. Maybe it's a neighbor or someone I may have met during the summer."

I noticed she was trying hard, stretching her neck to see it. She was curious but didn't want me to notice. When she saw that I did, she quickly turned her head away.

"Is there anything I can do?"

"Daisy could use a drink. If you could take her back to your house and give her one, I'd appreciate it."

Kneeling down she gave Daisy a pat on the head, then took the leash from me. Walking away, Daisy kept looking back whimpering, as if I had given her away. Seeing her upset, Veronica stopped, bent down once again giving her a pat on the head, just to reassure her that I hadn't.

Within a half hour, Officer Davis and a state trooper were coming over the walkway and down onto the beach. When they got to where I was standing, Officer Davis introduced me.

"This is Ron Bennett. He's the one who discovered the body."

"I'm Trooper Jesse Strange, New Jersey State Police. How did you discover it?"

"Well officer, it wasn't me who discovered it. It was my dog. She was exploring the dunes as she always does and called it to my attention. We didn't disturb the area, just phoned for the police."

He acknowledged my answer and then went over the sand dune with Officer Davis. They knelt next to the body, and I could hear them discussing the area's remoteness from the other houses along the beach.

I couldn't hear what they were saying, but after removing more sand, the face and almost the entire torso became visible. It was the body of a young woman. A pretty woman with long blond hair, that appeared to be in her mid 20's- a girl who tragically died far too young. Within a few minutes, two men in coverall uniforms came over the walkway onto the beach heading in our direction. One was carrying a folding stretcher, and the other carried a shovel. I assumed they were part of a team to take the body to the medical examiners lab.

When they got to where we were, they finished exhuming the body. Just as we thought, it was complete. Officer Davis was taking a long series of photographs to aid with his investigation during the entire process, while the state policeman was having a conversation with the people from the medical examiner's office. Officer Davis brushed the sand from between the fingers of the deceased and removed what looked like a sapphire ring. With both officers examining it, Officer Davis subconsciously read the inscription inside the band. "J.S. to K.W. with love." Then he placed it in a small plastic bag and marked it as evidence.

The State Trooper said, "Ben, that looks like the only physical evidence. It's going to be a tough identification unless she has fingerprints on file, or someone reports her missing."

"I know, Jess. First we'll have to find out the cause of death. From the marks on her neck, I think we can discount the idea she drowned."

I could see what he was talking about. There were extensive bruises visible around the neck, and what seemed to be a small open wound with traces of blood on the side of her head. I didn't see anything else that could have been used for her identification, and I watched as the medical examiner's team put the body in a bag and zipped it closed.

Like the final chapter in someone's life- zipped up into eternal darkness, never again to see the light of day, or know a quiet stroll along a sandy beach.

There was a small crowd of onlookers that gathered to observe the activity. They stayed until the body was removed and then slowly walked away talking to each other.

"Ron, could you come to the police station and give me a statement?"

"Sure, I'll be there as soon as I retrieve my dog. She's with Veronica, the woman who let me use her phone."

Ben stayed discussing the scene with Jesse. When I reached the walkway, I met Veronica. She was coming to see what was delaying me after seeing the men go by carrying the body.

"I saw them coming with the body. I asked them if I could see the face to possibly identify her. They unzipped it and I looked, but I didn't recognize her. I was wondering what was taking you so long."

"I was talking to Officer Davis and the state trooper. I have to go to the police station and give him a statement. Thanks for watching Daisy."

"She was no problem. If it wasn't for my husband Joel being so strict about having everything showroom perfect, I would have one myself. I already assumed you would have to give a statement. I was going to tell you she could stay here while you did, but when she saw you coming, she started pulling on her leash whimpering, trying to get to you as if she hadn't seen you in a month. I didn't want to upset her anymore, so I guess leaving her here would be out of the question. Are you a local?"

"No, I live in Philadelphia- Northeast Philadelphia. I come down to fish on the jetty at Holyoke Ave., about two blocks from here."

"I notice Daisy has all the sand brushed off her. That wasn't necessary. I always carry a brush and a drying towel in the trunk of my car for that."

"That's ok. I had an old hair brush and brushed her fur to calm her down. Besides, all ladies have to look their best, and she looks as much like a lady as any human. What's her blood line?"

"Daisy's part lab, part hound and part pointer- I got her at the Humane Society."

"I've never seen markings like that on a dog. They're unique, especially that brown heart on her head. Yes, she's definitely a lady."

As I was putting Daisy in the car, a green pickup truck pulled into the driveway. The bold lettering on the side door read, "Carl Dunn Builder Inc."

"Ron, this is Carl Dunn. He's the one who built the house. He's here to take measurements for a closet I want him to build in the hall."

When he stepped out of his truck, I could see he was a man in his early 40's with sandy blond hair and very muscular. He had on dungarees and a green plaid shirt. With the sleeves rolled up, you could see his thick forearms were use to doing heavy work.

"Good morning, Veronica."

Looking at my watch I noticed it was 10:30

"You're punctual as usual Carl. But you'll have to forgive me- I'm a little out of sorts this morning."

"Why, what's wrong? I hope it isn't something with the house is it?"

"No, this is Ron Bennett. He discovered, or should I say, Daisy dis-covered a young girl's naked body buried down the beach. The police just left with it about 10 minutes ago."

"Is it someone we know? Or someone who possibly drowned during the storm and washed up on the beach?"

"They let me look, but I didn't recognize her. If you were here awhile ago, you would have had a chance to look too. Maybe you could have identified her. The whole thing makes me unnerved."

"Was it an older person?"

"No, she looked like she was in her mid 20's. Wouldn't you say, Ron?"

"That's what I thought. She was very young."

"I saw Ben as I was passing him on the main road. I wondered why he didn't return my wave as he drove by. He usually does. I guess he has a lot on his mind this morning."

"Well, I better get to the police station and give my report. Then it's back to the city to write the article for the Evening Paper."

"So you're a newspaper reporter?" Veronica asked.

"Not exactly, I'm an investigative reporter. I work freelance. I don't like being tied to a desk permanently. Nice meeting you, Carl." I shook his hand. "When I become rich and famous, I'll look you up to build my home."

Carl chuckled.

As I got into my car, I could hear Veronica say. "I made a pot of coffee for Ron, but it's a little old. I'll brew a fresh pot for you."

Jealously surveying the job he did on Veronica's home again, I turned over the ignition and headed for the police station. It was in the Town Hall a few blocks away. Not a separate building, but a few rooms. I knocked on the door that had the word "Police Department." stenciled on it. A voice from inside called out- "Come in!"

Chapter 2

I entered the office, and the room was just as anyone would expect for an older building. The wood floors were bare and made a creaking sound as I walked across them. It reminded me of my elementary school of years ago- high ceilings with decorative lights suitable for an item in an antique store. Pictures of past city officials, dating back almost a century, adorned both walls.

As I entered the office, Officer Davis was awkwardly trying to cradle the phone under his chin, while trying to speak to someone, and writing at the same time. Waiting for him to finish his conversation- I began looking around the room. I saw a few diplomas hanging on the wall with his name and some community service plaques. There were also some old pictures of the island, showing extensive devastation done by past hurricanes. After he was finished typing his initial report he looked up.

"Have a seat Ron," he said as he pointed to a chair beside his desk.

"Ben, those pictures of the island are pretty devastating. When were they taken?"

"Some of them are pictures of Beach Haven after Hurricane Hazel in 1954. Some of the others I don't know. I found them one day while I was going through an old desk in the basement. They're a lot older. It's a shame no one ever bothered to date them."

He began the interview by asking me the routine questions: name, address and phone number.

"Do you live or own a house on the island?"

"No, I only come down to fish and walk the beach."

"What do you do for a living?"

"I'm a freelance investigative reporter for the *Evening Bulletin* in Philadelphia."

Looking up surprised, he said, "I've read a few articles you've written. They're pretty informative. How did you ever get in that line of work?"

"I was in the Military Police in the service and was assigned to investigative work- it seemed interesting, so I decided to take it up after I got out. Have there been any missing persons reported on the island lately?"

"No, but there are two sets of initials inside the ring band I took off her finger that might be useful."

"It looked like a sapphire. Was it?"

"Not being a gemologist, I believe so."

"The size of that stone on the ring, if it's real, it may be traceable to a jeweler."

"That's what I'm hoping. There's not much else to go on."

"Officer Davis, I'd like to stay in touch with you during your investigation, if you don't mind. If there's anything you can tell me without jeopardizing your confidentiality, I'd appreciate it?"

At that point, I think he realized the questioning *he* wanted to have, turned into an interview by *me*."

"Ron, call me Ben. I'll let you know anything I can without divulging something you shouldn't know."

"That's great, thanks."

After giving my statement, we shook hands. He walked me to the door, thanking me again for my help. After leaving the office, I headed back to the city.

On Saturday, I was reading the newspaper to check the accuracy of the story- then called Ben. They classified it as a homicide, which I already assumed, and according to Ben, they hadn't yet found out who she was.

The forecast was for nice weather all week, and I wanted to take a day off to go back to the shore for the surf fishing I missed that day. I had a Coast Guard receiver that gives constant information about wind and sea conditions at the shore.

It makes it an easy decision whether I should make the trip or stay at home. According to the Coast Guard report, today was going to be perfect!

Anxious to get going, I put Daisy, along with my tackle box and surf rod in the car. Banishing from my mind any thought of work or the city, we headed out for Beach Haven.

There are a few traffic circles on the way to the island, something New Jersey's famous for. At the last circle 30 miles from our final desti-nation, there's a convenience store that had become our regular stop. After getting a cup of coffee to go, and a treat for Daisy, it was back on the road. With the windows rolled down, Daisy occasionally put her head out, challenging the wind hitting her face. We continued our jour-ney, and after reaching the island, turned right and headed for Holyoke Avenue. It was my favorite jetty, and I had been more successful there than any other spot on the island. The traffic signals were all set on blink-ing yellow for the main road, and that was a sure indication the summer season was officially over.

Another regular stop before the jetty- was George's Bait and Tackle Shop on the main road. I've known the owner, George Hanson, for years. A heavyset chain smoker in his late 50's, he was an absolute encyclo-pedia when it came to sport fishing. When I walked in, he was talking to another surf fisherman, a person I wasn't familiar with. Daisy went directly to the counter and sat down watching George's every move. It was something that had become a ritual. She knew where the dog treats were in the large glass jar next to the register, and every time George moved in that direction, she stood up, tail wagging waiting patiently to be noticed. When he didn't call her by name, she would resume her prior position, like a sentry with a watchful eye.

"Hi, Daisy-- I see you. I know what you want."

Waging her tail seemingly knowing what he said, she patiently waited until he handed a dog biscuit over the counter. He gently patted her on the head, and she wagged her tail acknowledging his gesture, as if she was saying_ "Thanks for the treat." Then she began exploring the live bait buckets.

"Where's the hot spot for fishing George?" I asked as I looked over the fishing reels. I put them back when he finished with his customer and picked up some fishing hooks and line I needed.

As he was getting bait from the refrigerator, he commented, "They're doin' pretty good right out front."

"You mean Holyoke?"

"From what they're all telling me, all along the front, especially on the incoming tide." He said as he rang up the customer's sale and turned in my direction. The customer leaving turned and offered me useful information.

"If it's any help, they seem to be hitting on mullet or mackerel. I caught three fair- size bluefish from the beach yesterday right out front. That's where I'm headed."

"Thanks for the info, George. Give me some mullet and a mackerel."

Lifting the lid on the large chest freezer, he said, "I think I have a few left. They went pretty fast this week, as soon as the blues started showing up. Here- here's a mackerel at the very bottom. It looks a little freezer burned. It's probably from the spring run. I'm sorry- no mullet left."

"That's alright. I'll take the mackerel, the smellier the better. Blues don't mind. They go after anything." Picking it up from the counter, even frozen, I noticed it had a slight offensive odor.

"Smells like hell; but the fish love it. And Daisy certainly doesn't mind sniffing it."

Then I asked, "What's the word on the body that was found, anything new?"

"You tell me. Aren't you the one who found it?"

"No, it was actually Daisy." I said as I pointed down to her.

"Well, in that case, she deserves another treat."

She was familiar with the word treat and quickly resumed her position sitting in front of the counter, wagging her tail. George reached in the jar, leaned over the counter and gave her another. "Do they know who she was?"

"I don't think so. Ben told me he would stay in touch if he found out anything, and I haven't heard from him."

George chuckled. "Ben was in a month ago near the end of August. He said he was looking forward to the end of the season this year. I guess he thought with the crowds already gone- he was going to have it easy. He never thought anything like this would pop up."

Walking to the door I said, "Come on Daisy, time to hit the beach! George, if I get lucky, I'll let you know whether that customer was right about the bait."

"You do that. Bye, Daisy!" She looked back wagging her tail, seemingly sorry to leave.

When we got to Holyoke Avenue, I let her out then got my gear and went over the sand dune.

As I crested the top, I could see the ocean. The radio at home was right- the wind and tide were perfect. There was an older guy I knew named Tom coming off the jetty. I knew him from fishing here and a few other spots on the island. Surf fishermen, for the most part, are friendly and always exchange information on where the latest hot spots and what bait to use, like the guy in the bait store. Tom had a few nice fish, and when he stopped to break down his fishing rod and reorganize his tackle box, we exchanged a few words.

"Ron, are you the one who found the body of the dead girl?"

"Yes, what a tragedy, she was such a young kid."

"The paper said she was in her mid 20's."

"Yea, she looked to be about that- pretty girl, too!" Knowing he was a permanent resident, I asked, "Do they know any more about her identity?"

"I don't think so. It's a little upsetting having something like that happen so close to home too."

Shaking his head after he finished adjusting his gear, he acknowledged Daisy with a pat on the head, as she sniffed around his catch.

"Be careful of your footing out there. The rocks are wet and slippery."

"Thanks Tom, I'll be careful."

He wished me good luck, and I watched until he was over the sand dune and out of sight. Carefully climbing out on the Jetty, I baited my hook and cast out about 20 yards, where I knew there was a deep hole. I had been successful there before, and with the fish Tom had, I thought I could be just as lucky.

After jamming my rod holder between the rocks, I set my rod looking for a comfortable spot to sit. Not that rock's are very comfortable, but any discomfort is offset by the joy in just being out there fishing. For me, looking at the ocean is like a tonic- the waves washing ashore, sea birds soaring overhead and sandpipers running up and down the beach- really relaxing. I took heed to Tom's warning. Gazing out on the water, I remembered the day I slipped while out on these very same rocks. It all came back to me like a bad dream, reliving it as though it was yesterday.

Like today, the wind was from the ocean, and the water was choppy. It was late October and getting dusk. A guy I knew from being here before, warned me as he headed off the beach just as Tom had. Holyoke Jetty, as all the rest, is made up of black granite blocks, and set in orderly fashion when they're first put down. Over the years they settle differently in the sand, shifting and making what was once orderly, a contortion of rocks at different angles. This is caused primarily by the movement of the ocean, and the pummeling they get during storms. In time, like everything else, nature will prevail, and even the strength of granite rock, will eventually pulverize under constant pressure of the ocean, and Mother Nature's fury.

This particular jetty is about 200 hundred feet long and has a low portion in the center, probably 40 feet in length. If you're not attentive when the waves are windblown from the ocean, the rocks in that section are covered first, leaving you basically stranded. I was catching and releasing a few fish that day, far exceeding the safety margin of the water closing behind me. When I finally decided to leave, I made the mistake of picking up my rod, tackle box and fish bag before trying to negotiate my way back to the beach. I began to cross the water- covered rocks, cursing my decision to stay out so long. Trying to time the lowest point of the waves before moving forward, I wasn't making much progress. When I saw a wave coming in strong, I'd stop, and after the wave passed, would continue my slow walk.

I was already getting wet and knew I'd have to make the drive back to the city in relative discomfort. I thought to myself, only a few more feet, and I'll be fine. Just then, a rogue wave appeared, and I made a fatal mistake.

I tried hurrying over the remaining wet rocks to the safety of a higher one. When it caught me, the force of the water swept me off my feet, and I went down on my right side. The pain shot through me as I tried to catch my breath. No doubt about it, I knew immediately, having had the experience before, I fractured my ribs.

The waves were beginning to roll over me now at a steady pace, and as they passed, I had to hold my breath. The wind picked up and the water was rising faster than I was able to crawl. I was under water most of the time, and had to wait until they passed to raise my head so I could breathe. I had to stop periodically until the pain subsided again, before I could continue. With me being partially submerged, the wave action was pushing me off the jetty, and it was becoming difficult to keep my grip on the wet rocks. I had to make a decision- a quick decision, but a very necessary one. If you don't get the hell off this jetty, you may soon get washed off into about 12 feet of water. I had no choice but to abandon my tackle box and fish bag. I wasn't about to let go of my signature handmade 10 foot surf rod, or the Penn Reel attached to it. Somehow, I was going to save them.

If I can only get closer to shore, I could try to heave it onto the beach. Slowly, I painfully crawled to the higher rocks and was within throwing distance. Holding the rod like a javelin, I tossed it as hard as I could. The pain shot through my side again with that movement, and I had to stop again. Although I was on higher rocks, the water was still rising, but for the time, I was out of immediate danger. Crawling over the remaining rocks to safety, I finally reached shore. When I looked back, I saw my fishing bag and tackle box being claimed by the rising tide. Holding my side- I painfully made it over the sand dune to my car.

I thought to myself, "Damn, I hope I didn't leave my keys in my tackle box." Sometimes, I do. Luckily for me, they were in my pocket and opened the trunk to retrieve a blanket. Spreading it over the driver's seat, I drove a short distance to a department store on the island. The owner, Mike and his wife Ruth, I've known for years.

They've been very successful since purchasing the store, stocking items that pertain to the beach- suntan lotion, sun glasses, beach towels, beach umbrellas and toys for kids. It was about to close as I walked in, soaked and shivering, holding my side.

Coming out from behind the counter, Mike asked, "What the hell happened to you? Are you alright?"

"Mike, I slipped on the rocks. I think I fractured a few ribs. Can I get a dry sweat suit to get back to the city?"

"No problem, are you sure you don't want me to take you to the hospital? I'll drive you."

"No, for now it would be a big help with just a dry towel and some dry clothes."

After sizing me up for the sweat suit, he took them off the shelf. "Here, these ought to fit you. Take those wet things off in the dressing room and leave them on the floor. The missus will take care of them later."

Looking at me trying to open my wet wallet, to retrieve some water soaked money, Mike said, "Don't worry about that right now. You can pay me later. Just to be on the safe side, I wish you'd let a doctor take a look at that. Just stop at the hospital and get an X-ray, just to make sure there's no danger of a lung being punctured!"

"Sounds like a good idea."

He asked again as I walked to the door, "You sure you don't want me to drive you?"

"No, I'll make it fine. Thanks Mike. I'll see you next time."

"Remember, don't be a hard head! Stop at the hospital."

"Okay, Okay. I promise."

The drive to the hospital was short- just off the island. After getting X-rayed, the attending physician held them up to the light.

"You have three fractured lower ribs. Fortunately, none are complete separations. I'll have a nurse wrap your side with a large adhesive bandage. Take it easy for awhile- nothing strenuous, and try avoiding sudden twists of your body."

Getting instructions from the attending nurse, we struck up a conversation. Seeing she was without a ring on her finger, I asked for her phone number. It began a relationship that would eventually see her becoming my wife. That part of the experience seemed to have happened so long ago.

Suddenly slipping back to reality, I shifted my attention to what Daisy might be up to. Turning around, she was already busy exploring with her nose to the ground. In a few minutes, the rod tip started bending, and I knew I had a fish hooked. I picking up the rod from its holder and could feel the strain of the fish fighting against the line to get free. After surf fishing the amount of time I had, you can pretty much judge what kind of fish is on the line by the way the line and rod react. Tom had a few nice bluefish when he left, and I thought I might have one as well. After a few minutes, the fish came to the surface. I could see it was about a 6 pound bluefish. After landing it, I put it in my burlap bag.

Seeing more action on the water's surface, I quickly re-baited my hook and cast out in that direction. Swirls on the water generally indicated bluefish attacking a school of mullet, a small silvery fish that comes close to shore in late fall. Bluefish fatten up on them, as well as mackerel, while moving south to warmer waters. Within a few minutes, I had another strike. The rod bent violently this time, and the pull on it was noticeably stronger. I adjusted my feet so I wouldn't lose my balance, and the fish began to rapidly peel out line. The reel was clicking from the line being strained, then finally stopped.

The fish I already had- was about a 6 pounder. If this was another, it would have to be about 10 pounds, if not bigger. Damn, I couldn't believe my eyes. It broke the water and leapt into the air. I knew it was too heavy to pull up over the rocks, so I began making my way back to the beach. Reeling in every time the line stopped being pulled, I was finally able to negotiate my way back to the beach. I was still playing the fish, pulling on the rod then letting the incoming wave carry the fish inland, where I finally landed it. I was right- it was about 10 to 12 pounds- a really big one. It was a beautiful silver and gray fish, and in the sunlight when they're wet, they have a tint of green on their scales, looking iridescent.

A blue this big is referred to as a slammer. How or why they got that name is a mystery to me, but I wouldn't like to have my finger in its mouth when he snaps it shut- they close their jaws powerfully. It could also be that they're a carnivorous fish with a large head and sharp teeth. They've easily bitten through my 18 pound test fishing line with no problem.

Daisy was busy exploring until she saw me on the beach. Coming back to where I was standing, she greeted me and began sniffing the fish- jumping back when the fish moved, not realizing it was still alive. As I was putting it in my burlap bag, I heard a voice calling Daisy's name. She ran in the direction of a woman walking toward us, and I wondered who it could be. Coming closer, to my surprise, it was Veronica.

"Hi Ron, looks like you have dinner."

"Yes, I think for a few days."

She laughed as she reached down to pet Daisy, roughing her fur, as Daisy jumped around enjoying the attention. "How's my favorite girl today?"

She had a fine scarf around her neck, but with the breeze off the ocean, it partially uncovered what looked like bruises. I made no mention of it, but as she looked up at me, I think she knew I saw them, then tucked her scarf in a little tighter, then stood up.

"I saw the article in the paper with your name on it about the murdered girl. Have they found out any more about her?"

"Not that I'm aware of. Have you heard anything?"

"No, I did see a few posters with her picture prominently placed in different stores and restaurants on the island, though. They give a pretty good physical description of the girl. Maybe someone will see one of the posters and come forward. How long will you be staying at the shore?"

"I'm only here for a few hours, sorry to say. Why do you ask? You're not afraid to be alone since the body was discovered are you?"

"No, my husband and I are having problems. I just wanted to get out of the city for awhile."

I think she was trying to tell me that's where the bruises came from without actually saying it, so I pretended not to notice.

"I'm sorry to hear that. Does he come to the shore often?"

"Yes, when he's in the mood, which isn't very often with me lately, sorry to say."

I think she was telegraphing to me the message that Joel's interest was waning for whatever reason, and she was troubled by it. I thought to myself, "Could it be a physical problem on his part? Men do have periods they go through. Is he older than her? If he is__ how much older?" There was nothing I could see about her that wouldn't excite any man's passion. I had a strange feeling that it wasn't the end of the conversation.

Looking down, she began toeing the sand as if she was contemplating whether she should speak. Suddenly, like a dam that burst, words just seemed to start flowing from her mouth. She looked at me as if she was angry for some unknown reason.

"We had an argument when he found out from a neighbor you were in my house having coffee."

Was it this that was troubling her?

Surprised at the near accusation I asked, "An argument with who__ your husband?"

"Yes, I tried to explain to him what happened and even showed him the article in the newspaper."

Feeling a sense of rage that I was the catalyst causing her grief, I abruptly replied, "What did he do then?"

"He said he didn't want to hear it; he cursed at me and called me a liar. When I told him we could go to the police station, the officer who was here could probably explain it to him, he really got angry. For some reason, when I mentioned the police station- he really got mad. He was still calling me a liar, walking around me in circles, waving his fist in my face, accusing me of all sorts of infidelities. I was really scared. I've seen him angry before, but never like that.

He really scared me. When I told him to calm down, that's when he grabbed me by the neck and pushed me down on the couch. He's extremely jealous."

I was right. Out of her own mouth Joel was responsible for the bruises I observed on her neck. Still bent down arranging my fishing gear and getting ready to leave, I looked up. "He sounds like he's not only jealous, but a little dangerous too. Do you want me to tell him what took place? Give me your phone number. I'll call him."

Looking at me with a less- accusing smile, she said, "No, I'd rather you wouldn't right now. If he brings it up again, maybe I'll ask."

Seeing the marks on her neck, temporarily my thoughts went to the girl on the beach. The marks I observed around her neck were similar. Was it coincidental? -Maybe. This is only our second meeting. We hadn't known each other long enough to get into personal conversation, yet I felt a compelling interest to let it go on. I guess its part of a prerequisite for writing newspaper articles. The urge to get the full story is strong.

"My husband Joel called a little while ago, he said he wants to come down later to apologize and take me to dinner."

"Well, you're telling me this just happened recently?"

"Yes, the day before yesterday. That's why I took a walk on the beach. I really don't__" She paused, looking down at my face, then continued. "I really don't want to be around when he gets here. I just may head back to the city and stay with a friend for a few days, just to think things over."

She continued volunteering information that I thought was a little personal for only being our second encounter, but realized she had quite a bit of pent up emotions and wanted an ear to listen, so I obliged.

"Does he come down often by himself?"

"He's been coming down for about a year- maybe a year and a half- since we've been having problems. Sometime, he'll come down with one of his personal secretaries. Here lately, at least two or three times a month."

"Secretaries, that's plural. He has more than one?"

"Yes. He has a large staff. He gets them all from a temporary agency in the city. I don't know for sure, but I think he must be hard to work for. They never seem to stay with the company for more than a few months. When I questioned him about it, he said it was because he wouldn't have to pay them health care. The health care issue would be between them and the company that supplies them."

"Does he come down with them, taking a chance he'll run into you?"

"No, and even if he did, I've never had that kind of suspicion when it came to our relationship, I trusted him. He came down with the latest secretary it seemed like once a week- more so than any of the others. For some reason she stopped coming. When I asked why, he told me she just suddenly quit."

"Did you ask why she quit?"

"No, like I said, he must be a hard person to work for. If he's as demanding in his business as he is with his home, I can see why they don't stay. He feels he has to maintain control. I don't see any other reason for them to leave. He pays them well enough."

"How long has it been since the last one left?"

"About three or four months, I think it was her__" She paused then continued. "I think it was the argument about me finding a set of women's underwear in the trunk of his car. We had a severe argument over it, and I think that's why she left. Either that, or Joel just released her, thinking that would solve the issue of me no longer trusting him."

I thought to myself __"Well that's understandable I'd say it's also a sufficient path leading to grounds for a divorce."

She realized she was divulging more pent- up feelings than she thought was appropriate and changed the subject.

"Where do you live in the city?"

"I have an apartment in the Northeast."

"That's right. I think I asked you that question before. I notice you don't have a wedding ring. I take it you're single."

"Yes, my divorce was amicable though. We just seemed to live in two different worlds. I think the feeling was mutual, so we just separated at first, then, just never got back together. The only commitment I have now is Daisy."

"She doesn't mind if I invite my friends over to watch a football game." I said with a smile. "In fact, she enjoys the extra company. She loves potato chips, and once in awhile one of my friends will give her one."

Smiling at the comment, "I'll bet she gets a lot of attention when their around too; she seems like a really great dog."

"Yes, she sure is good company."

She replied, "I sometimes think I should have stayed single for awhile, but Joel was kind and gentle in those days, so I agreed to marry him. I don't think my poor mother liked the idea very much."

"Why's that?"

"He's 10 years older than me."

"That's not that big of an age difference. Besides, as you get older, that distance between your ages will seem insignificant."

"I don't think it was that alone. He made it plain from the start he didn't want children, and my mother couldn't understand why. Knowing how he has to have everything just so, a child around the house would be something he wouldn't like.

I wouldn't want a child to be constantly under pressure that way. The problems we're having now, is probably a second good reason not to have had a child. This change in our marriage is getting a little out of hand."

Without me realizing it, she put me right back into her personal life's trials. Now, I thought the conversation was really getting a little too personal and dropped the questions. This time it didn't seem to make a difference. She kept going- reeling me in, just like the fish I just caught.

I felt she was looking at me, as if I were a marriage counselor or domestic court judge, someone who was going to render a decision in her favor if her defense was strong enough. Realizing I hadn't commented on her confession, she continued.

"When I confronted him with it, that's when our relationship really started to change."

I was nonchalant about her comment, still straightening my tackle box, as though I wasn't paying attention, but I understood exactly what she was saying- every word of it. Acting as though I just became aware of her comment I asked. "Confronted him, confronted him about what- the secretaries?"

Suddenly making a fist and placing the back of it to her mouth, she seemed to bite her lip, fighting to hold back tears that began welling up in her eyes.

"No! No! The underwear I found in the trunk of his car. Don't you understand? __The underwear I found in his car!" She turned away, trying not to show me she was so desperate to let out her feelings- she was almost crying.

Realizing how upset she was and not being able to help was the worst possible feeling. There were always limitations to circumstances I encountered on the job, but here on the island with her being so upset, for some reason, bothered me more. Do I ask her to take a ride with me to the other end of the island and just listen over a cup of coffee? I didn't know what to do. I really didn't want to get between two married people. I knew better. I covered several stories before where a wife killed a husband and vice versa. With her, somehow I felt different. Was it a physical attraction? Could it be that it was taking place on the island- the island that I love so well? I didn't know, but I realized the interest was definitely there.

"Look, Veronica, is there anything I can do? Finding that sort of thing in the trunk of his car would certainly have cause for a heated argument. If you feel that way and it's something you feel you can't reconcile, why don't you just get a divorce?"

Regaining her composure, she turned around to look at me. "Since his money provides us with the lavish lifestyle I've grown accustomed to, I always found it difficult but tolerable.

I can put up with his little idiosyncrasies- like having everything always showroom perfect or his spontaneous outbursts over his work. But being physically abused, I can't tolerate. At this point I just don't know what to do."

In an authoritative voice, I replied, "My suggestion to you is be careful. That's what you should do. If he gets more abusive, I'd leave and get a restraining order."

"Maybe you're right. It will give me something to think about over the next few days; that's for sure."

"I'm sorry, Veronica. I'd love to stay and listen, but I've given you my best advice. I have to get going, I have a corruption story I'm working on, and have to get back to the city to finish it. The deadline is due before midnight."

Wiping the tears from the corner of her eyes with one end of the scarf, she said, "I understand. I'm sorry I ruined your few hours at the beach with my problems. If we meet again, I'll try to do better."

She knelt again to ruff Daisy's fur. "And how's my favorite lady doing today? Did you enjoy the beach? You're so cute! Hand me her leash Ron, I'll walk her to your car."

When she knelt down to attach the leash I could see more of what she was trying to hide with the scarf. The bruises weren't from just being pushed down on the couch, as she claimed. They looked as though he was trying to strangle her, but again, I made no mention of it. She walked out to the car with me, holding Daisy's leash while I carried my fishing gear and catch. After putting my things in the trunk, I retrieved Daisy's hair brush and began to comb out her hair. After finishing, I opened the door and put her in the front seat. Quickly turning around, I caught a glimpse of Veronica wringing her hands in desperation. I sensed immediately, she didn't want me to leave. Was it because I was a good listener?"

"Goodbye. Thanks for walking Daisy to the car. Remember what I told you about a restraining order, especially if he gets violent again. I hope everything works out."

As I was getting in the car she appeared to be nervous, urgently wanting to ask me another question but not quite sure what my answer would be.

Realizing her anxiety and wanting to ask, I hesitated after getting into the car to give her that opportunity.

"Ron:" She paused__ "I don't want you to think I'm too forward, but could I have your phone number?"

Surprised, I suddenly looked up, hesitating to give her an answer.

"What, my phone number at the newspaper office?"

"Yes, if you don't mind, just in case." She paused- "Just in case I have a problem with him about you being at the house. Remember, you said you would call if he's still upset about it?"

Again, I knew it was bad policy to get between two married people, but for some reason, I abandoned my own caution and decided to give it to her anyway.

"Okay." She seemed temporarily relieved as I opened the glove box, to retrieve a pencil and paper. After writing down my phone number, I handed it to her.

"Here's the phone number of my cubicle at the newspaper office. Glancing up I said, I also wrote the phone number of my apartment too. If it's an emergency, don't hesitate to use it, I'm generally home after six."

She looked at the phone number, clutching it to her chest as if it were a life ring thrown to someone adrift at sea. Would it help her with her crisis? Only time would tell. Her hand was still on the door with my window down, as if she was pleading, "Please don't leave."

Realizing there was nothing further I could do, I turned the ignition key and the motor turned over. "Well, goodbye again."

After patting Daisy on the head once more, she slowly drew her hand away, stepping back. She remarked, "Good bye pretty girl. I wish I had someone like you to protect me."

Protect her, protect her from what? That thought immediately registered in my mind as I rolled up the window then slowly pulled away. Looking back through the rear view mirror, I could see her put her hands to her face, as if in desperation. She couldn't hold back her feelings any longer, and began to cry.

I was almost at the end of the block when I hit the brake. My first thought was to put the car in reverse and go back. I felt guilty, as guilty as if I abandoned someone who was in desperate need of help- a truly hopeless feeling. I would no more abandon a person like that, than I would drive by a pregnant woman standing alongside the road with a flat tire. Disturbingly, I thought about it all the way home, trying to justify my actions of not going back. If her abuse means less than the luxury of the lifestyle she's enjoying, that's her decision; a foolish decision, none the less, but hers, and only she has the power to do something about it. She's a beautiful woman and has what seems to be a nice personality. Hopefully her situation will work out.

Chapter 3

Two days later, I walked with Daisy to the convenience store around the corner from my apartment. It gave Daisy a breath of fresh air, and I'd get my usual coffee and newspaper to go. When I got back to the apartment, I opened the paper to check if my last article about a union dispute wasn't screwed up by a misprint. What really caught my eye; was a small article on the second page. It was another corpse that was discovered on a vacant lot, right next to George's Bait and Tackle Shop.

"Holy Shit!" I exclaimed- they found another body- Near my peaceful fishing spot too."

Intently, I read the article. I knew the property. The lot had been empty- for all the years I had been going to George's. It was sort of an unofficial overflow parking lot customers used when the store lot was full. The article explained that someone recently purchased it to have a new home built. The excavator found the remains as he was digging the foundation, and the authorities believed it to be a young woman. It mentioned that it had possibly been there for at least four to six months.

Hmmm! Four to six months. I thought about what Veronica told me when she said her husband was coming down with his secretary, and her suddenly quitting about five months ago. I wondered if there was a connection between the body I discovered on the beach, and the body mentioned in the article.

From the marks on Veronica's neck, and what she told me about her husband's temperament, I was becoming more concerned about her safety. Both bodies were within close proximity of her home. I remembered how anxious she was for me to stay, and with this new discovery, became anxious for her to call.

Was my mind running away with itself? Maybe she hadn't seen the article? If she calls I could tell her about it. I also wanted to know if there was any change in her relationship with her husband.

Almost a week passed without word from her. I thought- either they worked things out, or she left him. I felt a little better about what I resolved in my mind and decided to let it go.

I finished my corruption story and was basking in the light of possibly a notable mention, when it came to the Pulitzer Prize- not that I set my expectations too high. I was at a standstill for another story to cover, and wondered if a trip to Long Beach Island would lead to another major story.

There were two bodies found. Maybe it's a serial killer? I wondered if the officer I met the day I found the body was on duty. I remembered his name. It was- now let me see. I sat there clicking my pen against my chin. No: too much on my mind. I think I have his name in my desk from the article I wrote. Opening the desk drawer moving things around, I was searching for his card. Yes, here it is. Officer Ben Davis. He seemed pretty professional. Maybe he wouldn't mind sharing some information with me on the discovery of the latest body. After I leave the office, I'll pick up Daisy and drive down. Maybe I can dig up a story. Dig up a story- now *that's* appropriate wording.

Getting back to my apartment, I popped a dinner in the toaster oven then fed Daisy.

"Wanna take a ride?" She looked up at me, wagged her tail and headed for the door.

They say some dogs are very intelligent, and I think mine was at the head of the class. As a friend of mine once said after being in her company observing her response to words, "This dogs definitely, no dope on a rope. She's smarter than some people I know."

After Daisy and I ate dinner, we headed out.

I didn't know whether the police station was even open. In some small townships, the police go home and conduct any business via police radios installed at their residences. Pulling up in front of the town hall, I saw the lights on at the police station. I parked the car, and entered the building. I could see only darkness in the other offices I passed, with the exception of the police department. Approaching the door, I heard typing from inside. Hesitating at first, then I knocked.

"Come in!"

When I opened it, Ben was doing the typing and immediately rose from his desk... "Hi, Ron- I guess you already know we unearthed another body. Do you have anything to add to my report?"

"No, I was wondering, did you get any identification on the girl from the beach?"

"Yes, we were able to find out her name was Karen White. She lived in Philadelphia and worked for a temporary personnel agency. That's about it."

"What's the name of the temp agency?"

"Wait a minute. I have it written down here. It's Webber and Associates Personnel Services... 1212 Chestnut Street, Philadelphia."

"Where did she live, in the city?"

"She has an apartment in the Northeast section of the city, but she's originally from Scranton. That's where her family lives. They haven't heard from her since last time she was home, about a month ago."

"Then that would make it about two weeks before she was killed."

"That's right. When I questioned them about the ring, they didn't seem to know anything about it. They never knew she may have been seeing someone on a steady basis. After I described the ring, they said they never saw her with it. I mentioned to them it looked like an engagement ring and asked if the other set of initials, J. S., meant anything to them, possibly someone from her past."

"Well- Did they?"

"No, they called back and told me they contacted all of her friends, and they couldn't match up the initials either. They even went through her high school graduation book without any success. They said when she last visited she wasn't wearing it and never mentioned being engaged."

"Ben, it's a possibility she may have gotten engaged between the last time she was home, and her return to Philadelphia. Either that, or she didn't wear it when she was home and never told them about it."

"No, they're certain she would have mentioned it. As far as they know, she wasn't even dating anyone. I kind of got the idea she was a free spirit. They didn't seem to want to get into a conversation about her past."

"When you say *free spirit*, you don't mean she was morally corrupt, do you?"

"No, I just didn't want to question them about it, and they didn't seem to want to volunteer any information."

"I hope they claimed the body after the medical examiner was finished his forensic work. Did they?"

"Yes, they came down right away, I was told."

I thought about the secretary whom Veronica said went missing and knew from her that she was a temp who worked for her husband Joel. Damn- Damn. That's right! Veronica said her last name was Simmons. J. S. Joel Simmons. Could it be a coincidence? Don't kid yourself. It's no coincidence, it all adds up. The initials are the same; the close proximity to his home; the fact she worked for a temp agency.

I didn't want to tell Ben what I suspected. If I was wrong, no harm done. I did want to talk to Veronica first, just to find out if she knew more about the agency. Maybe Ben could take a trip there for an interview. Maybe he could follow up on the other missing secretaries who suddenly quit. Maybe they quit in the same manner? Not wanting to confuse his investigation, I kept what I suspected to myself.

"Ben, I saw the article in the paper about the body you recently discovered. That tackle shop is my regular stop for bait. What the hell's happening to this place?"

"I don't know. I don't think there's ever been a homicide in Beach Haven. Now it appears we have two."

"I wonder if the two homicides are somehow connected."

"We haven't gotten the results back from the one that was decomposed at the vacant lot. That will take several weeks. But the one you discovered on the beach died of strangulation."

"I already suspected that."

"Get this. The toxicology report read that she had an overdose of chloral hydrate in her system."

"What the hell is that?"

"According to the medical examiner, it's a drug that was used in small doses for insomniacs as a sleeping potion, and that's not all. It's colorless and odorless."

"That sounds to me like it would be the perfect potion for putting in someone's drink."

"That's just what I was thinking. The medical examiner told me an overdose would put the victim in an almost comatose state, rendering them pretty much indefensible. An overdose would be fatal."

I remembered the ring being a blue sapphire and thought to myself, they don't come cheap, especially with a stone that size. It had to be at least 10 karat weight.

"Do you know where the ring was purchased? If you could find the jewelry store, they would probably have the name of the purchaser." I was concealing my knowledge of the initials J.S. inscribed inside the band.

"We have a detective already checking jewelry stores in the tri state area. Why all the questions? Are you personally interested, or is it professional journalism?"

Pausing, not knowing whether to divulge Veronica's problem, I decided to tell him it was the latter. "For now Ben, let's just say its professional journalism." Pausing for a few seconds, I thought for Veronica's sake maybe I should say something?"

"Ben, the truth is I'm concerned for a female friend who lives nearby. She's been having marital problems with an abusive husband."

"Now, you're being mysterious. Is it separate from this homicide investigation, or just a separate domestic problem between husband and wife?"

Did I say too much? Maybe I should have just kept my mouth shut. He pressed me further for her name, but I replied, "I don't think they're related.

But she's very much afraid of him, and I'd like her to tell you about it. I'll try and get in touch with her. I haven't seen her for awhile. She may have left him already. I really don't know. She was talking about it the last time I saw her. I'll tell you what. If she wants to speak to you about it, she'll have to be the one making that decision.

"Fair enough- If she wants to talk, I'd be interested."

He handed me his card with his name and the phone number of the police station, and I put it in my pocket. "Thanks Ben. I'll be seeing you."

I left the office and slowly cruised past Veronica's house, straining to see if there were any vehicles. I didn't see any parked outside, but I didn't know whether there were any in the garage. Some lights in the living room were on, but with no cars in the driveway, I assumed they may be lights that were on timer switches.

After slowly going by, I sped up and parked at Holyoke Avenue, then opened the door for Daisy. We walked over the sand dunes and down onto the beach. There was almost a full moon, and although it was a little chilly, the reflection on the water was gorgeous. The light from the moon shining on the phosphorus in the water seemed to highlight the top of each wave, riding its crest almost all the way to shore. The sound of the small waves lapping against the sand made the night picture perfect.

I thought to myself, "Damn, wouldn't it be nice if I ran into her?" Did I say that out loud? I hope there was no one else on the beach. They might think I was crazy talking to myself.

Daisy ran down the beach to stretch her legs, and I just took a leisurely walk along the shore line, enjoying the night. I thought to myself that Joel must not know how lucky he really is. He has a gorgeous home at the shore probably one just as nice in the city. He more than likely has a ton of money in the bank, a beautiful wife who obviously has a talent for interior decorating, and a knack for keeping it looking great. What more can a man want?

Still wishing I would see her, I was beginning to realize, in just a few short encounters, that she was like no other girl I have ever known before. She was someone I was really beginning to have an interest in. I knew it wasn't just her situation but something inside, something much deeper.

Was I falling in love? Impossible, we only had two encounters and they were under stressful situations. I imagined they would have been a lot better if they weren't.

After about an hour, I went back to the walkway leading over the dunes to where I parked. I noticed something under my windshield wiper. What could that be? Looking around, it couldn't be a ticket. I was behind all the signs for "No Parking." As I looked at the paper, knowing it wasn't a ticket, my heart began to race. It could only be from one person; the person who's been consuming most of my thoughts since we last met. Quickly brushing the sand off Daisy, I got in the car. Fumbling, trying to turn on the inside light, I opened the note. Yes, it was from her. Making sure I absorbed each word to get their full meaning, the note read, "It was such a beautiful moon. I wish we could have met. Please call me during the day tomorrow."

In one line it sounded romantic, and the next line read like a plea, as if she was desperate. A plea- and I didn't quite know what to make of it. Am I reading this right? Let me go over this again. Did it read what I thought it read? Yes, at the bottom it says, "Love Veronica." That's an endearment. When I saw her phone number at the bottom of the note; my heart raced. Folding it again, I put it the glove compartment.

Quickly getting out of the car, I went over the sand dune, thinking I might get a glimpse of her still on the beach. I waited for at least 10 minutes, but no such luck. I retreated back to the car. Still encouraged by what I read, I wondered why she didn't just call during the week. I gave her my phone number for the office and my apartment. Maybe she lost it? I told myself, "Don't speculate. She wants you to call- that's a positive."

Driving by her house again, straining to see if there was any activity outside- but there was none, and still no car in the driveway. Did she leave? Was she there with Joel? If she is, maybe she wants to tell me they've resolved their issues. On the other hand, why the- "Love Veronica" at the bottom of the note? Did she want to start an affair to get even with an unfaithful husband?

On the way home, I wondered why she didn't just come down on the beach if it was something that urgent. If she didn't know which direction I went, she could have just waited by the car for me to return. Maybe she just wants to talk?

She did ask whether I was married. My mind was letting my expectations run away with itself. Hopefully she was just as interested in me as I was beginning to be in her.

When I got to my apartment, the light on the answering machine was blinking. When I hit the play back button, the call was from Veronica.

"I'm sorry I missed you at the beach, it was such a beautiful moon. I would have enjoyed walking with you. By now I know you got my note. Call me tomorrow morning at 10 o'clock- ten o'clock sharp."

I couldn't get her out of my mind, something wasn't quite right.

The whole thing was going too fast, but I desperately wanted the conversation- not only to see or hear from her again, but to warn her about the second body that was discovered, if in fact she didn't already know. Anxious to make the call the next day at exactly 10, I patiently waited- 9:50 come on hands, get moving. I checked to see if my watch had stopped; no it's still working. Finally 10 AM: I quickly dialed the number. The phone was picked up before the second ring, which was encouraging. I told myself she was waiting patiently for my call and had to be sitting next to the phone when it rang.

"Is there a place we can meet?" She said in a whispered tone.

"I'm at work right now, but I'll be able to meet with you after I'm finished."

She paused. "Ok, what time will that be?"

"I leave here around 4:30. I have to go home first- change clothes, feed Daisy, and take her for a short walk. Where do you want to meet?"

"Could you meet me on City Line Avenue at the entrance of Lord's and Logan's department store? Make it the main entrance."

"It'll take me a little longer with the traffic that time of day. I'll probably get there between 6 and 6:15."

"That's fine. I'll be waiting."

I thought to myself, "How appropriate, Lord's and Logan's. Where else would she shop? Only the finest:"

She sounded anxious, and I wondered about the spot where she wanted to meet, and why so clandestine.

"You sound upset. Is something wrong?"

"I'll tell you all about it tonight when I see you."

I began to speak when her conversation ended abruptly, when I heard the receiver click. I had expected at least a few more words of conversation, but there were none. I was disappointed. She was gone.

Anxiously waiting for the end of the day at 4:30 sharp, I hurriedly turned out the desk light then left my cubicle. Arriving home, I quickly changed clothes and took Daisy for a short walk.

The traffic was heavy that time of evening around City Line Avenue, and I arrived at the mall later than expected, around 6:30. Walking in through the main entrance of Lord's and Logan's, I began scanning the room looking for her. She came out from behind a rack of women's dresses. Like a deer being stalked, cautiously eyeing the area for the dreaded hunter, she approached me.

"Why the caution, has something happened with Joel to make you so afraid?"

I didn't know, but by her actions; all of a sudden my defense mechanism kicked in. Her fear became contagious, and my defensive instinct for a potential confrontation followed. From which direction would the threat come from? I didn't know that either, but I wanted to be prepared.

Grabbing me by the forearm she asked, "Could we find a quiet spot where we can talk?"

I repeated myself anxiously wanting an answer, "Why are you so afraid? What's wrong? Do you want to leave here?"

"No, it's more crowded for our safety."

Now my defense instincts were really in high gear. I always carried a derringer when I was on assignments that placed me in a questionable position, but I never expected this kind of scene. The weapon for my safety was still snug in the top drawer of my dresser. Great! That's just great! I suddenly felt naked and defenseless.

She kept looking around as if she was being followed. "There's a small restaurant in an alcove right off the main thoroughfare of the mall. Let's go there."

When we entered the restaurant, she quickly scanned the room checking to see if there was anyone she knew. There weren't many patrons, and after examining the premises, realizing we were safe. We took a booth in the back where she positioned herself, so she could see anyone entering the restaurant.

I hoped this meeting is the start of an affair, and all this caution was only concern, she doesn't want to be seen with another man- a man other than her husband. It couldn't be. All this dramatics wouldn't warrant it. The last time we were together she wasn't on the greatest terms with her marriage, so it has to be something else. I gave her my undivided attention. As she spoke, I realized it wasn't for the purpose I anticipated. It was a fear of something, or someone, and it began to make me even more uncomfortable.

The waitress came to the table, and I ordered two drinks.

"What would you like?" I asked.

"I'll have a Cabernet."

"Ok. Make mine a Merlot."

After the waitress left the table, Veronica began to speak. I interrupted...

"Why didn't you wait for me at my car? As you said on your message on my answering machine, I'm sorry we didn't meet. It was such a beautiful moon. What gives?"

"Forgive me Ron. I was very upset. I waited at your car for what seemed like hours, but after I got back to the house, I realized only 20 minutes passed. I received a phone call yesterday from a private detective."

"What did he want?"

"He said he was looking for a missing girl. One of his leads was a check stub from Joel's business. It was cashed five months ago."

"Why should that make you so upset? You suspected he was seeing, or had been seeing someone."

"No, let me finish. The name he gave me was the same initials on the underwear I found in the trunk of Joel's car."

"What did you tell him?"

"I told him he would have to contact my husband. I don't have anything to do with his business."

The waitress returned with our drinks, and after she walked away, I thought it was a perfect opportunity to ask. "What business is Joel in? Why should you be afraid?"

"His father was a wealthy stock broker in center city; he had high-end clients. With no other children when he died, Joel inherited everything. I'm beginning to think there's more to Joel going to the shore house with his secretaries. I hate to pre-judge him, but he may be the one responsible for their disappearances!"

"You saw the face of the girl on the beach. You said you didn't recognize her. Were you hiding something from the police then?"

"No, I don't always get to meet them. He changes secretaries pretty frequently. If she was one, she couldn't have been there for more than a few months."

"How often does he change them?"

"It seems like every three or four months. The last one was there the longest. I'd say about five or six months. This whole thing is like a bad dream. It's bazaar."

"That phone call by the detective- Was he suspicious of Joel about her disappearance?"

"I don't know. I don't think so. But I found out how Joel knew you were at the house having coffee with me. He said a neighbor told him, but that was a lie. I spoke to her. She told me she never spoke to Joel about it. In fact, she said she hasn't seen or spoken with Joel since late summer. It has to be from someone who's been following me- maybe a private detective or something. I always knew he was a little jealous, but I never thought he'd stoop that low, having me followed."

"Maybe that's why he was angry with you the day you had the violent argument. Not that it gives him justification for hitting you, or rather, choking you. I saw the marks on your neck the day you saw me on the beach. It wasn't from just being pushed down on the couch, was it?"

"Actually no, I didn't think they were that visible."

"Well, they were. You don't realize how helpless I felt leaving you that day. It bothered me. I mean *really* bothered me. I asked you if you wanted me to call him and straighten it out- remember? Why didn't you let me? I knew you were really upset. Maybe getting a call from me would have solved some of your problems."

"Even if you would have straightened it out with a phone call, it still means he's been having me followed for awhile, even before our first encounter. I don't know how long it's been going on."

"Maybe it's been since you found the underwear in the trunk of his car. He may just be having you followed; trying to build a case of infidelity against you, just in case you decide to get a divorce. You know, preparing a counter punch for whatever you have against him."

She quickly snapped back, "Infidelity?" Me? I never thought of that. Maybe you're right."

Captivating my mind through this conversation was a deep concern for her safety. With all the events in the last several weeks, circumstantial or not, things were beginning to point to Joel as a bigger problem than she was suspecting- and I pried a little more.

"Have you ever given serious thought about leaving him before things get worse and possibly you becoming a victim? If you have, my apartment is available to you if you need a temporary escape." I jokingly added, "Daisy won't mind another lady in the house."

She looked surprised at my offer- then smiled.

"I don't want to make my problems something you have to deal with. But thanks anyway."

Suddenly I became serious. "In case you haven't noticed, I'm already involved."

My implication at this point- and I hope she understood that clearly- was not just professional, but a relationship I wanted to begin.

After finishing our drink, we left the restaurant and got to a spot we couldn't readily be seen. I was hoping for a gesture of endearment- a light peck on the lips, or a reassuring hug- but she cut my enthusiasm short.

"We shouldn't walk out together. I parked at the other end of the mall, just in case I was followed... I'll be in touch."

I waited about 15 minutes then left through a different door. I was disappointed that we couldn't enjoy a few quiet minutes together, but I knew, this is only the third time we met, and it's always been under a stressful situation. If it wasn't for that, we may be enjoying a different kind of relationship. My concern was a little voice in the back of my mind saying, "I hope the next time you see her pretty face, it wouldn't be as a missing person, or in the newspaper obituary column."

When I returned to my apartment, the answering machine light was blinking. I hit the playback button, and it was Ben. I returned his call immediately, and another officer picked up the phone. "Beach Haven Police Department: Officer Kevin Jones speaking. How may I help you?"

"Is Officer Davis there?"

"No, he's out on an assignment. Is there something I can help you with?"

"Ben wanted to talk to me. I'll call back later, thanks."

I left the apartment to take Daisy for her evening constitution. The whole time I was walking her I was thinking about my conversation with Veronica, and wondered just how much she would take before going to the police. When I returned home, I called the Beach Haven Police Department again. Ben answered the phone this time, and after he gave his name, I identified myself.

"Ben, this is Ron Bennett. What did you want to speak to me about?

"I wanted to tell you we've found another body on a vacant lot- not very far from where you discovered the first one. It's in a pretty advanced stage of decomposition and probably been there for about nine months or more. This body, like the last one, was discovered by Ed Johnson, an excavator who found the last body. He was digging a foundation on a vacant beach front lot, where a new home is going to be built."

Surprised at what he was telling me, I couldn't contain the concern for Veronica's safety any longer.

"Ben, I think it's time to let you know about a woman who has a house in Beach Haven. It's close by where I found the body on the beach. She has an abusive husband, and I'm afraid for her safety."

"You mentioned that before. Do you want to come down and talk about it?"

"No, not until I contact her first. I'll call her tomorrow and ask."

After hanging up, I assumed with the fear Veronica was showing this evening, it wouldn't be a problem for her to go with me. The next day I called the newspaper and spoke to my editor Lawrence Clark.

"Lawrence, this is Ron. I'll have to put the latest corruption story on hold. I have to take a trip to Beach Haven this morning."

"Is it about the bodies being discovered?"

"Yes, I got a call last night from the police. They've discovered another body yesterday."

"Another one: Then by all means go. It's beginning to sound like a serial killer."

He already knew I found the first body, and knew there had been another discovered since then. The island was in a grip of fear, and the police department was under severe pressure to find an answer. This recent find would only make it a lot worse for Ben and the department. Since I worked mainly freelance for the newspaper, it may be an addition to any news I could glean, and Lawrence didn't have a problem with it. I called the number Veronica gave me at 10: AM: the same time she had given me before. I assumed it was a time that would be safe, possibly a time when Joel would have already left the house. When the phone rang, she answered immediately.

"Hello Charlotte."

"No Veronica. It's me, Ron. How are you this morning?"

It was obvious by the tone of her voice the phone call was unexpected.

"I'm still upset. In fact, I called my girlfriend earlier. I thought this might be her returning my call."

Not telling her about the recent discovery of a body, I was adamant with her. "I'm taking you to the Beach Haven Police Department this morning. What time and where can I pick you up?"

"Why? I had other plans for today. The friend who's calling me is the real estate agent. She's supposed to show me an apartment."

"Forget about that today, damn it! Look, you're going with me. I refuse to take no for an answer."

She hesitated, contemplating an answer. After a few moments of silence, I repeated myself, "Damn it, you're going with me. I think you may be in more danger than you can imagine. Now- Where can I pick you up?"

ing lot. That would be best. I'll park at one end, walk through, and come out the front exit at Lord's and Logan's, just in case I'm being followed."

"Good, I expect to see you in about 40 minutes."

I knew my phone call was a surprise, something totally unexpected, but was happy she finally agreed to go.

The traffic around the mall is always a little heavy due to all the offices and shopping centers, and pulling into the parking lot, I quickly swung by the entrance. Seeing my car, she hurriedly exited the store and I threw the door open, letting her jump in.

I stopped at the exit of the parking lot, waiting for the traffic that was stopped to resume again. Timing my exit to a short break between cars, I darted out into traffic with a narrow safety margin from the next oncoming car. I just made it, and as expected, got a horn, then a raised middle finger from the car behind me. Traffic was heavy but moving fast. Without a doubt, if anyone had been following us, they were left behind.

"What's wrong Ron? Why the rush; what happened?"

"Well, you started with the concern about being followed, and I didn't want anyone to know our destination if you were. There's been an additional development at the shore. Even if you're not going to remove yourself from the potential danger of being in Joel's company, I am."

I couldn't contain it any longer. "Ben, the policeman that you met the day I found the body on the beach, called."

"What was it about?"

"They found another body yesterday afternoon in the same area. He wanted you to come in and tell him about Joel."

She seemed surprised. "Did you tell him about what we've been talking about?"

"No, but I think you should tell him about what you're afraid of, and the physical abuse he's done to you."

Remaining quiet, she didn't have the panicked look she had the evening before, when she thought she was being followed. I wondered why?

When we got to the island, we went directly to the police station. After knocking, we stepped into Ben's office. He got up from his chair and said hello.

"I remember you. You're the one that let Ron use the phone the day he discovered the body on the beach." He extended his hand to shake hers.

"I remember you telling me you and your husband were friends of Carl Dunn and his wife Carla. Please, sit down," he said pointing to a chair next to his desk.

"Ron tells me you've been having domestic problems. Would you like to tell me about them?"

Taken by surprise, she looked inquisitively at me; realizing I lied about divulging any of her problems. She was annoyed, but didn't comment.

Ben began to question her. "What's your husband's name?"

She interrupted.

"Officer Davis, what I say here isn't going to leave this room, is it?"

"Not unless you want it to. I take it you only want this interview to be confidential. Do you want Ron to wait in the other room?"

Smiling at me she said, "No he can stay. In fact, I'd rather have him here. He's been so helpful."

"I promise whatever you say in this room, will stay here."

"For now, that's the way I want it. My husband's name is Joel. Joel Simmons."

"Where do you live?"

"We live just outside Philadelphia, right off City Line Avenue near Saint Joseph's College. We also have the property on the beach where I first met you."

"How long have you been married?"

"Ten years. Yes it will be our anniversary in December- December 31st. We decided to marry on New Year's Eve."- She said getting off the subject.

Getting right to the point, Ben asked, "When did he begin to abuse you?"

"He began to get abusive when I discovered some women's underwear in the trunk of his car and confronted him with it."

"That's understandable__ Oh! Sorry for the interruption."

I believe Ben let that one slip. He had the same thought I had when she told me, but probably wouldn't have wanted his inner thoughts aired during the interview.

Ben continued... "How long ago was that?"

"It was a little over a year ago."

"Was it a physical confrontation?"

"In a way__"

"What do you mean in a way? Did he strike you?"

"No, he grabbed me by the neck and flung me on the couch."

"Had it ever happened before?"

She looked at me then cast her eyes toward the floor, realizing I knew the answer to that question, and had to tell him the truth.

"Yes, several times."

"How many would you say?"

"Only a few, it didn't really get bad until about nine months ago."

"How many times has it happened- as you put it- before it got really bad?"

"About four times, my husband is really possessive and jealous."

"What does your husband do for a living?"

"He's a stockbroker in Philadelphia. He owns the firm."

She told him about Joel's business and everything else, for the exception of one small point- and the most important one, I thought: Bringing the secretaries who worked for him to the shore house- then after awhile, their sudden disappearances.

As I listened to the answers she was giving, I realized all she was doing was giving direct answers without elaborating... generic answers.

Answers that weren't inclusive, of her private thoughts about Joel possibly being a serial killer. I thought it was strange she didn't mention the phone call from the private investigator trying to track down a missing girl. Why didn't she? Why didn't she mention the detective telling her the name on the pay stub was the same initials as on the underwear she found stashed in the trunk of his car? If she suspected Joel, why didn't she tell him about all this? Perhaps, she didn't want to go as far as accusing him of murder, at least not at this early stage.

When she finished giving Ben the answers to all his questions, she stood up to leave. I picked up her jacket holding it open so she could slip it on, pulling it up over her shoulders. "Thanks Ron." She said looking over her shoulder.

She looked at Ben. "Officer, you promise this interview won't leave this room?"

"No it won't leave this room. Are you sure you don't want to press charges?"

"No, I don't think so, at least not at this time."

"If you decide to change your mind, here's my card. It has the phone number on it. Goodbye Ron. Thanks for bringing her in."

After we walked out of the building, I asked, "Why didn't you mention the initials C. A. on the underwear you found, matching the initials on the pay stub the private detective inquired about?"

"If Joel's having me followed, I was afraid he could just as easily have someone come after me. For now, I just want to play along as though he wasn't aware of what I suspect, at least not just yet."

"That sounds a little dangerous to me, like playing Russian Roulette, never knowing if the next time you pull the trigger will be fatal."

She became sharp with me. "For now Ron, that's the way I want it."

"I hope you realize what you're doing. You're jeopardizing your safety."

She seemed to want to change the subject, and I let her.

"Ron, if you don't mind, I'd like to stop for something to eat on the way back. I didn't have a chance to eat this morning. I was supposed to go to breakfast with my friend. I don't think she's going to appreciate me standing her up. You sounded so urgent when you called; I didn't want to waste any time. I never had a chance to call her and cancel."

"It's a little too late for breakfast. Would lunch be OK?"

"That sounds good to me."

Chapter 4

We pulled into restaurant about 15 miles from the island. Claxton's Log Cabin Restaurant has been a landmark fixture since the early 1900's. It's a popular eatery that boasts an all-varnished pine log exterior and interior, and the bar sections are made out of thick pine that's heavily varnished but has darkened considerably with age.

The area's now referred to as the Pine Barrens Wildlife Preserve- an expanse of hundreds of square acres consisting mainly of small pines and scrub oak shrubs. More than likely, it was also a source of material to build Claxton's. During World War One and World War Two, the barrens became a training ground for the Army. Barracks were hastily erected and large numbers of young men made the transformation here from civilians to soldiers. The bar is adorned with the assorted military patches of different units that had been going through training or stationed here over many years.

With a little imagination, you could close your eyes and envision all the enlistees in the smoke- filled room- crowded around the tables and bar on liberty, drinking and talking about the war and their unit's destination after training. Letting your imagination enter that world of long ago, you could almost hear singing by troops in various stages of inebriation. World War 1, with "Pack up your troubles in your old kit bag and smile- smile- smile." or one of the popular tunes from World War 2, "Chattanooga Choo Choo, Wontcha' Choo Choo me Home." Home: That's where I'm sure they would have rather been.

The stone hearth fireplace with the ornate wrought iron ends compliments its rustic beauty. When we were seated near it, the warmth from the fire immediately took the chill from us. I always liked Claxton's because of its atmosphere. The quality of the food, whether it was lunch or dinner, was always exceptional. When the waitress came to our table, I ordered a dry wine for myself and remembered Veronica liked a Cabernet. After the waitress walked away, I was toying with a book of matches, the complimentary kind with the restaurant logo, and asked__ "What's your next move with Joel?"

"Before I do anything to arouse his suspicions, I'm going to inquire about getting my own apartment. I told you that's why I was meeting my friend this morning."

Looking bewildered at her answer, I asked in a loud, annoying tone, "Don't sound crazy. If he's having you followed, wouldn't that be something he'd notice- you looking for an apartment?"

My voice was rather loud and the waitress came to our table to ask if anything was wrong. After I told her everything was fine she walked away.

Veronica continued, "My friend has already shown me a few. We have similar tastes, and she's keeping an eye out for something I might like around City Line Avenue."

Becoming more annoyed with her seemingly disregarding her potential danger, I remarked in a loud tone, "Are you kidding me, thinking about living in the same area?"

The waitress returned once again to the table and asked, "Are you sure everything's alright?"

"Yes, were fine. I'm sorry I raised my voice, I promise I'll be quieter."

Veronica continued, "I'd like to live there. Everyone I know is in that area, and it's convenient to shopping at the same stores I'm familiar with."

Thinking it was a good time to ask, wanting her address, "Just, where do you live?"

"We have a house just off Route One near Saint Joseph's University."

I already knew that from the interview with Ben. Prying a little more, I asked, "What's your home address?"

"710 Lincoln Drive."

Making a mental note of it, I asked, "I take it Joel has an office somewhere?"

"Yes, his offices are in Center City. He has two businesses. He also keeps an apartment just off City Line Avenue in the Adam's Tower's Apartment Building. I'm sure you've seen it."

"Yes, I sometimes go to the sports bar just down the street from the T.V. Studio. I have some friends who work there, and we generally try to meet for Eagles or Flyers games. What's Joel's other business?"

"He has an investment firm that backs developers."

We paused briefly when the waitress returned with our drinks. We waited until after she took our food order, and departed before continuing our conversation.

"You know Veronica, sometimes it's better to cut and run in a situation like this. You're not dealing with someone that's normal. If he thinks nothing of strangling a person- or persons, which seems to be what it's shaping up to be- he may eventually decide to get rid of you too. In several cases I've been involved with where people have been strangled, there's always – and I mean always- evidence of a struggle. Not to be too upsetting__. The person who has the ability to look someone in the face as they struggle for breath, watching life ebb from their eyes, has to be the coldest of cold- blooded murderers. That's a person who's capable of doing anything. I know by now you must realize I care for you more than just someone who's having marital problems. I don't want you to laugh at me, but this feeling I have for you is real- very real. Something I haven't felt for a very long time. I__"

We were interrupted as the waitress came back with our order. I thought to myself... "That was perfect timing for her not to have to make a comment on my last question." After the waitress left, I began to speak again. "Let me continue where I left off."

Reaching across the table, she placed her fingers gently over my lips. I made a kissing gesture on her fingertips then she smiled. Pausing for a moment she seemed to be gathering her thoughts about how she was going to answer my question. I waited patiently.

"Ron, I've never known a person who was so sincere. Believe me when I tell you, if it wasn't for the situation I'm in, our relationship would be a lot more intimate. Trust me, after I straighten things out with Joel, then I'll be able to concentrate on a relationship. Right now, there's just too much going on in my life."

Feeling better about my position, I relished the fact that she was thinking of her future- and the possibility of including me in it. I still had one overwhelming concern- The thought that she may yet be a victim and it was continuously haunting my thoughts.

Not wanting to be redundant to the point of frightening her by constantly talking about the horrible danger she might be in, I forcefully said, "Look, Veronica. For the last time, just so you understand, I'm worried about you."

Not knowing for sure, but I think I was right about not frightening her with my warnings. We began small talk about likes and dislikes, and I sensed our light conversation took our minds temporarily off her immediate problem.

As we were leaving, she commented to the waitress, "I often passed this place but I've never been inside. I'll be sure to come back again."

Walking to the car in the cold air as the wind was blowing, she pulled the collar of her unbuttoned coat closed and held onto my forearm. I opened the door for her then briskly went around to the driver's side.

After getting in, I rubbed my cold hands together. Unexpectedly, she grabbed the collar of my coat, jerking my head around to meet her awaiting full, voluptuous lips. She delivered the most passionate kiss I ever experienced, and I didn't want it to end. To my surprise, she must not have either, she didn't fight my advances. Cupping her breast, even with the bulky sweater she was wearing, it felt firm in my hand, and seemed to arouse a passion in her far too long subdued. The more I explored, the more passionate we became, which drove me further into something I desired from the minute I laid eyes on her.

I felt her hands pulling at my sweater- then running them up under my T-shirt, and scratching at my back. I took a chance by letting my hand slide down between her legs, and she separated them slightly. Running my hand up to the top of the zipper of her Jordashe Jeans, I slowly slid it down, running my hand over her flat stomach.

I began trying to explore her a little deeper, and she didn't seem to fight my advances. With each move, we seemed to become more passionate, and the kiss seemed like it would never end. I could feel her nails scratching deeper on my back and thought for a woman in her late 30's, she was alive- very much alive.

Maybe this is what Joel failed to do? It certainly felt as if she had pent up passion waiting to be released.

I noticed a person coming in our direction and suddenly stopped. It didn't seem to affect her, and she continued unabated. The man got into a car next to mine then drove away. I didn't want another untimely interruption but didn't want to continue in the middle of the parking lot. Although there weren't that many more cars, the end of the parking lot was more secluded, so I stopped for the moment to move.

I wished I thought ahead and pulled to the far end of the lot from the start. I couldn't second guess it now. It was too late. She lost the moment. I knew I temporarily blew something that was totally spontaneous, but it was something I really wanted since the day she almost begged me not to leave.

"Do you want to stop at my apartment or go to a motel? There's several back on the island or a few on the way back to the city?"

Kissing me lightly on the lips, "Believe me, I want this as much as you, but I want the timing to be right. I don't want it like this, not for our first time."

"You're right. It's just that I was surprised and got caught up in the moment. If I offended you, I apologize."

"You don't have to apologize, but let's wait. When it happens, I know it's something I'll really enjoy."

Disappointed, I got out of the car and straightened my clothes, worrying whether she would think of me as a teenager and not more sophisticated the way she thought I should be. When I got back in the car, she seemed to be still coming down off her passionate mood, a mood she couldn't fake. Yes, she enjoyed it as much as me.

After zipping up her jeans and readjusting herself in her seat, we drove back to the city in relative silence. I began to think her words were just to keep my confidence. If not, why the silent treatment?

When we arrived at the mall, I parked opposite from where she parked that morning.

Thinking she may have been disappointed and didn't know quite what to say, I wasn't going to let her out without a few more words of apology. She had her hand on the door handle and was about to get out when I began to speak. Suddenly, she grabbed my collar, turning my head just as she did in the parking lot at Claxton's. This time she only caressed my face, then gave me a light kiss on the lips.

"Goodbye Ron, Don't worry. I'll be in touch."

It was so different from the passion I experienced on the parking lot at Claxton's, and hoped it wasn't a kiss off.

After I got home, Ben called.

"Hello, Ron. I wanted to ask you something. Did Veronica leave anything out of her statement? I don't think she was telling me the whole story. I didn't say anything at the time, but Joel Simmons- J.S. -those are the same initials that were inscribed on the sapphire ring."

Not wanting to divulge more than what she already told him, I acted as though I never thought of it.

"You know, Ben, that's right. Maybe I should call her, and tell her about it?"

"I wouldn't do that just yet. Why make her more afraid? It sure looks like there's a connection between that body and her husband though. I just may bring him in for an interview, but she doesn't want her interview brought out in the open."

"I know. That's what's bothering me. Do you think you could convince her otherwise? I'm getting a lot of pressure to get this thing resolved. People here are really scared."

"I don't know whether she'll do it Ben. She's still pretty upset. She's been upset for the last few weeks. Something like that may just put her over the edge. At this point I don't think she'll even listen to me. I had a hard enough time getting her there for the interview."

"I imagine she is upset. Her husband doesn't sound very stable. Why doesn't she want to prosecute?"

"I'm not sure. She said she enjoys the life style her husband can afford. Sounds a little crazy to me, doesn't it?"

"It sure is. I want to ask you another question you may know the answer to. Do you know whether she has any knowledge about the dead girl on the beach being employed by her husband?"

It was getting on touchy ground, and for some reason, I found myself defending her from his question.

"No. I don't think so." …But in my mind I wondered. If she did, why didn't she say so?

"The medical examiners report I have in front of me reads she also has chloral hydrate in her system and was probably dead, or close to it when she was strangled."

"Were the other bodies checked for the same substance?"

"The third body was in an advanced state of decomposition, so a test for chloral hydrate may not be possible."

After hanging up, I tried to call Veronica to bring her up to date on what I just learned, but there was no answer. I decided to take Daisy out for a much- needed walk. With everything going on, I'd been a little lax in my attention toward her. I was about to step out the door when the phone rang. I quickly answered, hoping by chance it was Veronica.

It only rang three times before I picked up the receiver, but all I could hear was a dial tone. Whoever was calling either changed their mind, or it may have been a person realizing they dialed a wrong number. Maybe it was her, and she was interrupted by Joel suddenly coming home, and forced to hang up. I waited for 20 minutes before leaving again.

Giving up on a return call, I took Daisy for her walk and anxiously returned to the apartment. Walking in the door, my eyes immediately focused on the answering machine. No luck. The phone call that was missed wasn't returned. It would remain a mystery.

Several days passed without a word from her- no phone call, nothing. I found myself constantly anticipating hearing her voice every time the phone rang at my cubicle at the newspaper.

Every day when I got home from work, the first thing my eyes focused on was the light on the answering machine, only to be disappointed when the message wasn't from her. Did I get the kiss- off the day she got out of the car? It seemed as though it was. I was annoyed with myself for screwing up the start of what might have been a great relationship. If only I could have had a little restraint. I screwed up. Yea, Ron you screwed up big time.

Finally passing it off as an opportunity missed, I got back to work in earnest on another corruption story. I had fallen behind after several days of trying to keep a relationship going that wasn't really there, and told myself it was only a mirage. Several more days passed, and it was becoming easier to get back to my normal routine without flogging myself for screwing up.

"Hey Ron, you got a phone call while you were out to lunch."

"Male, or female?"

"Don't get excited. It was a man. He was a cop from Beach Haven, I wrote his number down. It's on your desk."

"Did he say what he wanted?"

"No, he just left his number. He wants you to call him back."

"Thanks, John!"

Hearing the shock of his words, I could feel my heart begin to race, and suddenly, a churning feeling in my stomach. Was I about to jettison the lunch I just finished? For days- I'd been annoyed with the reason she hadn't called, was because she was disappointed with my action on the parking lot. Thinking to myself, you selfish bastard, maybe it wasn't her fault after all. But maybe her failure to call was something more frightening. Was Ben about to tell me they found another body- hers?

I hurried to my cubicle and picked up the note. It was from Ben. I dreaded to make this call not knowing what he was going to say. I hope like hell it's not going to be bad news, like finding Veronica's body. Picking up the phone, I quickly dialed the number.

"Is Officer Davis there?"

"Just a minute: Hey Ben! It's for you."

"Hello! Officer Davis."

Excitedly, I asked... "Ben, this is Ron. Ron Bennett. You called. What's it about?"

"I haven't heard from you in about a week. I wondered if you ever got a hold of Veronica Simmons."

A sudden feeling of relief came over me, and my stomach began to settle down.

"Ben, you don't realize the anxiety attack you just gave me. I dreaded calling you, fearing you were going to tell me you found another body- hers. Tell you the truth Ben- I haven't seen her since the day I dropped her off. I tried calling a few times, but it's a situation where I can't leave a message."

"I suspected you two were an item. Was there a problem bringing her in for the interview?"

"No, not really: We said goodbye to each other in the parking lot, and she said she'd be in touch, that's all. I thought it was just the end of a relationship, but now, I'm not so sure. I know where she lives, but I've never been to her house. We always met at a mall on City Line Avenue."

"This relationship you have- It's something that's just begun then?"

"Yes, it sort of happened after the day I first met you. In fact it was over her husband being pissed off."

"Pissed about what?"

"About me being there having coffee the day I was waiting for you. She told me he found out about it, and accused her of possibly having a relationship with me."

"You mean by just calling the police and waiting for me to arrive? Sounds like he's a little bit of a control freak?"

"Yes, she told me some of his weird habits, like constantly asking where she was and who she was seeing. She even told me in her own words, 'He has to have everything show room perfect all the time.' How would you like to live with that anvil around your neck?"

"I wouldn't! Look Ron, if you hear from her, let me know. The mayor is breathing down my neck about getting this thing resolved. The pressure's really on."

"Will do, Ben in fact, I'm going to call her after I hang up with you. I'll pretend I'm someone else, and leave this number. If she recognizes my voice, maybe she'll return the call. Either way, I'll keep you informed."

Hanging up the phone I tried to think of how I would present the call without bringing suspicion of who I was, just in case Joel happened to answer. I dialed the number.

"Hello the Simmons residence. Who's calling?"

The voice was a female, and I assumed it was a servant or maid or possibly just someone from a cleaning service.

"This is the circulation office of the *Evening Bulletin* are you the resident?"

"No, I'm the maid. How can I help you?"

"Well, is there a member of the family there?"

"No, Mr. Simmons isn't home yet, and Mrs. Simmons is at their shore house. What do you want?"

I repeated again, "This is the circulation office of the *Evening Bulletin*. We're interested in expanding our circulation in your area. Do you get the *Evening Bulletin* delivered?"

"Yes, we just started to get it a few weeks ago. They already get the *Inquirer*. I sure don't know why they needed another one."

I laughed. "If I can call back later, what would be a good time?"

"Mr. Simmons usually gets home before 5:30. That's when he usually eats dinner."

"I wouldn't want to disturb him then. When will Misses Simmons be home?"

"I don't know. She's been at the shore house for two days now. She sometimes stays there a few days, sometimes a whole week. She didn't rightly tell me when she'll be back!"

"Thank you. You've been so helpful."

"Do you want to leave your phone number? I'll have one of them, give you a call."

"No, that's quite alright. I'll try again tomorrow."

"Well, if you're going to call, make it before 9:30. That's when Mr. Simmons generally leaves."

She told me all I wanted to know. That's why Veronica had me call at exactly 10. She's at the shore, and she's still alive thank god. I'll drive down as soon as I'm done at work. Maybe I can see her.

Four- thirty couldn't get there soon enough, and when the hour arrived, I hastily headed straight for the elevator. Getting home in record time, I quickly changed clothes, fed Daisy, and headed out the door.

We made our regular stop at the convenience store, and missing dinner, I grabbed a quick hot dog and coffee to go.

Going over the causeway bridge, I wondered if I might have passed her on the way back to the city. Never mind that. At least you know she's still alive. As I passed the Town Hall, I could see lights still on at the police department. Ben must be still working. I slowly rounded the corner on the street where Veronica lived. There were a few lights on, but no car in the driveway. I decided to go over the walkway at Holyoake Avenue a few streets away and down on the beach.

The night air was considerably cooler than the last time I was here, but in spite of it, I braved the elements. There wasn't a cloud in the sky, and it seemed as though a million stars were spread over the night sky like a canopy. Daisy ran along the beach and began her usual activity, exploring the dunes for anything she could find.

Some of the houses along the beach were in complete darkness, while a few seemed alive with lights from inside. Occasionally I would get a whiff of smoke from a lit fireplace in one of the houses. When I got to Veronica's it was lighted, and I strained my eyes looking for any activity of shadows on the closed drapes.

Was she home? Were the lights on timer switches? Enough with the examination: Should I just go up and knock on the damn door? No, I don't want to do that. Maybe Joel's there. Maybe he came down after he left his office?

I was just about ready to turn and walk away when I saw headlights entering the street. Wait a minute. Is it Veronica coming home? Maybe she went to the store or was out to dinner.

No, it's a pickup truck. Maybe it's Carl Dunn. She said he and his wife were friends. Maybe he's just stopping for a friendly visit? Well, in any case, I don't want to disturb them.

Disappointed, I called Daisy then headed back to the car. At least with his visiting the house, it too confirms she's still alive.

After brushing Daisy off, I decided to stop at the police station. Walking down the darkened hall, I was just getting ready to knock when I heard two voices from inside. They were discussing the victims, and seemed to be in an argumentative tone. I listened.

"I think we should just send this Joel Simmons a message to come in. We can tell him his wife came in to talk to us about his abuse, but fell short of pressing charges. If he is the one, maybe it will shake him up? We have to do something. We're getting a lot of pressure. The public's scared. We're at a dead end here."

I heard Ben's voice responding__ "I know Kevin, but the only thing we have to go on is his possible connection with the secretary's employment at his company, and the initials on the ring. Besides, I took

Mrs. Simmons's statement on a completely different matter. I told her I wouldn't act on it unless she asks me to. Other than that, there's no probable cause."

"Well I think we should pursue it from the angle of knowing the ring was purchased by him at that jewelry store in the city."

"Wait a minute. Just hold it right there. Number one, the jeweler said it was ordered by him but was picked up by a woman, remember? It could have been another secretary or even Karen White, the victim. We don't know. The jeweler didn't remember what she looked like, and there's no way to connect him with it. Number two, leaning on the slim chance the initials are his. There are plenty of people with the initials J.S. They might just stand for John Smith- or even Joe Shmmo for that matter. We're on the right path. We just have to find a way to connect the dots."

It seemed like the conversation was over, so I knocked.

"Come in!"

"Hi Ron, what brings you to the island? This is Officer Jones, Kevin Jones. Kevin, this is Ron Bennett, he's the one who discovered Karen Whites body."

Looking at Kevin and sizing him up by what I heard through the office door, in my mind, it was a pretty accurate picture. About 25 years old, six foot two inches tall, thin with blond hair and a little frustrated by his own impatience. He looked at me then replied… "Glad to meet you!"

Picking up his cap and putting on his jacket, he sarcastically remarked, "Ben- I'm going on patrol. Maybe I'll find a clue we can use. You know, to be able to connect the dots." Frustratingly shaking his head, he walked out the door. Ben acknowledged his sarcasm with a wave of his hand.

"Ron, do you have anything to add to this mystery?"

"Other than what you already know, no, nothing. I haven't heard from her in awhile, so I posed as a sales person for the newspaper and called her home, trying to make contact."

"Well, did you?"

"No, but I did find out from the maid that she's been down here for several days, and that's what brought me here."

"Did you talk to her?"

"No, I went by the house, but I didn't see any activity. As I was leaving, I did see a pickup pull into the driveway. It looked like it may have been Carl Dunn's."

"Carl Dunn's truck:"

"Yes, that's what it looked like. Well, there's nothing more I can do here. I'm heading back to the city."

"If you contact her, try to convince her to press charges. That's the only way I can see this thing going forward, and that's a slim shot."

"Not that I was listening at the door on purpose, but I heard the conversation you were having with Kevin. He's right about one thing- a slim chance, but it might just shake him up. Well Ben, I'll keep in touch."

Getting back to the city, I fell back into the routine of gleaning news for my corruption story. As the days passed without hearing from her, I was beginning to think she was having reservations about a relationship with me.

If the maid gave her the message, I wondered if she would, as Ben said to Kevin, be able to connect the dots and call me. Maybe the maid only told Joel, since Veronica was at the shore and never mentioned it to her? It wasn't a message that anyone would feel had to be passed on or discussed. Besides, the maid told me they were already getting the edition.

At the end of the week I sort of gave up on the idea and put it out of my mind. I was no longer captivated by looking at the light on my answering machine, to see if the much desired phone call was recorded. Getting ready to take Daisy for her evening walk, I was about to open the door when the phone rang.

"Hello, Ron Bennett, who's calling?" there was no answer. The call was still live, but whoever was on the other end, wasn't responding to my question. I waited for a few moments. "Hello, can I help you?" still no answer.

"Look, if this is a joke I'm hanging up."

A quiet voice finally responded, "Ron Bennett. No, this isn't a prank."

The voice wasn't familiar, and I didn't know whether it was someone connected to one of my corruption stories. I've had threatening phone calls in the past making me unnerved, but it was all part of the job. He knew my name and phone number and I felt that was getting too close to home.

"Who is this?" I demanded.

"Could you meet me at the Halftime Sports Bar on City Line Avenue? I want to talk to you."

I still didn't recognize the voice to be one of my friends.

"Who the hell is this?"

"This is Joel. Joel Simmons, Veronica's husband."

A shock went through my body, and my heart began to race. I could feel my face getting red and the hairs rising on the back of my neck. Gathering my composure I replied... "I can be there in about an hour."

There was no further conversation. All I could hear was the buzz of the phone after it was cradled.

I stood for a few moments staring at the phone, wondering how he got my number. I realized he either found the paper I gave Veronica with my number or someone that was following her saw me. If that's the case, why didn't he just come here to confront me?

I grabbed Daisy's leash and headed out the door. The whole time walking her, I kept wondering how he got the number. I realized one thing- the fears of being followed were no longer suspicions; they were real. I quickly returned Daisy to the apartment, and had my hand on the doorknob, getting ready to head to our meeting, when I suddenly stopped. Not wanting to be caught without protection, as I feared that night when I met Veronica at Lord's and Logan's, I went to the top drawer of my dresser and retrieved my derringer, putting it in my pocket, just in case.

Chapter 5

I knew the sports bar and had been there many times. I had friends who worked a few blocks away at the local T. V. station, and sometimes our work crossed paths, especially with the news people. Sometimes, we would gather at the bar for Flyers and Eagles games. The Eagles were playing tonight, and I knew it would be crowded- a perfect place to meet, crowded for my safety.

All the way there, I thought about how I was going to handle this encounter. Would he be hostile? If he knows my phone number, does he know what I look like? Does he know what kind of car I drive? Maybe it's a setup, and as soon as I get out of the car, someone's going to gun me down in the parking lot? I thought, "You're starting to think a little mellow dramatic, aren't you? Why not wait until you get there and find out.

Pulling into the parking lot, I found an empty space. Not wanting to pull in forward, I backed in. I wanted to scrutinize the area just to see if anyone was standing around, looking like they were waiting for me.

I waited for about 10 minutes but didn't see anyone. Just in case, let me check my gun to make sure it's loaded. A naked feeling swept over me. I never examined it before putting it in my pocket. Nice time to think about it, I thought. The same feeling of unpreparedness came over me as it had the night of the clandestine meeting with Veronica. I checked- feeling relieved- yes it's fully loaded.

After exiting the car, I stood looking around for a few more minutes waiting to see if someone would approach. No luck. He must be in the bar. After walking in, I stood at the doorway for a few minutes scanning the crowded room.

Monday Night Football was on T.V. the *Eagles* against the *Giants*... an away game at the Giants stadium. Every time there was a touchdown scored by the Eagles, the crowd at the bar erupted in chants- Eagles! Eagles! Eagles!

One of my friends Allen, who was standing at the bar, recognized me standing by the door. He approached, annoyingly putting his arm around my shoulder. He was already half way to his maximum capacity with alcohol, slurring his words and masking his normally impeccable linguistic talent.

"Hey, Ron: How ya doin' old buddy? We're sitting at the far end of the bar over there. He pointed in that direction. Where you been keeping yourself? I told the guys if you haven't been here for the games, you had to be pretty busy. You here for the game tonight? It's only the first quarter. The Eagles are ahead 14 to seven. Come on, I'll buy you a beer."

"No thanks. I'd like too, but I'm supposed to meet someone here that I never met before."

Quietly, as if he didn't want to blow my cover, he asked, "You mean some real secret squirrel shit? Good luck if you're taking a confession wearing a wire. This wouldn't be the right spot for quiet tonight. It's as noisy in here as two skeletons humping on a tin roof."

"No Allen, In fact, I'm glad there are so many people."

Looking a little confused, he began to walk away.

Turning again, he said, "Well if you finish with whatever interview you have, why not join us."

Just then, Charlie, another friend who works with Allen, recognized me and came over.

"Hey Ron, you here for the___"

Allen cut him short, putting his forefinger to his lips. "Shhhhh___"
Putting his arm around Charley's shoulder, he pretended to look suspi-
ciously around. Escorting him back to the bar, he turned and whispered
again, "Shhhh. ___Ron's here on assignment, let's not blow his cover. We'll
be reporting it on the seven o'clock news tomorrow night."

They both chuckled as they walked back to join the crowd. Just
then a tumultuous cheer went up from the patrons: "Yea, Eagles! Eagles!
Eagles!" they must have scored again. No wait. They intercepted the ball.

When the crowd subdued, there was a patron standing at the bar
that didn't seem interested in the game. Could this be Joel? I think it
is. He cast a wary eye in my direction and after a few minutes, realized I
wasn't joining my friends and approached me.

Eyeing me up and down, he seemed to be taking stock of me as
if I was an automobile he was about to purchase, but wasn't quite sure. I
could have made book on him, realizing I was examining him the same
way.

Like two rams getting ready to square off over mating rights, he
asked, "Are you Ron Bennett?"

I answered in a challenging tone. "Yes, if this is about being at your
house on Long Beach Island, I'd like to clear something up right now."

He didn't give me a chance to finish but looked around the room
for a quiet place to talk- then pointed to a booth in the corner.

"That looks like the quietest spot in here. Do you mind?"

"No, that seems like the best place to talk. I'm going to order a
beer. Do you want one? I'll have the waitress bring it to the booth."

"That sounds good!"

Walking behind him, I was still sizing him up as we wound our way
through the crowd to the corner.

After taking off his long cashmere coat, I thought, "He'd have a hell
of a time overpowering me." He didn't look at all physical. A thin man
about 6 feet tall in his late 40's, he had sharp features and receding gray
hair. He looked like a person who would be in the command of a broker-
ing business or the head of some other financial institution.

He had a smooth way about himself and displayed an air of confidence. If I didn't know better, it appeared as though he was getting ready to speak pleasantly to a perspective client, rather than getting ready to have a conversation with someone he thought was having an affair with his wife.

"Am I interrupting a night out with your friends?"

"Not really. They work for the T.V. station down the street. Work wise, I have contact with them from time to time. We get together here once in awhile for a few beers and watch a game."

"I guess you have contact with them about news articles?"

Quickly responding, I asked, "How did you know I was in the newspaper business?"

"To be honest, I didn't. I've seen Ron Bennett on a few newspaper articles and just put two and two together. I saw the article you wrote about the girl on the beach and the corruption story you just did. It just so happens, I know something about the story. I'm familiar with the guy they arrested. He was once a client of mine, Howard Krass. I always thought he had some sort of shady dealings. I've suspected it for awhile. He seemed to have a constant supply of money coming in with no real connection to any kind of business."

"Joel, I want to explain the reason I was having coffee with Veronica in your kitchen. After I discovered the body, she let me use your phone, that's all. She did ask if I wanted a cup of coffee until the police arrived, and I accepted. I'm sure you can check it out with the police. Oh, and another person you can check it out with- your builder, Carl Dunn- he was arriving just as I was leaving."

"Carl- Carl Dunn?"

"Yes. As I recall, he was coming to take measurements for the extra closet your wife wants him to build."

"What closet?"

"I don't know. Why don't you ask your wife? Didn't she tell you about it? I distinctly remember her saying, "Carl, you're punctual as usual." Still a little nervous with my conversation, I repeated myself, "I distinctly remember her saying that. I glanced at my watch when she did. It was exactly 10:30. Like I said, he was arriving just as I was leaving."

"I didn't know. I'll have to speak to her about it."

"Is that all you wanted to know? I asked her to give me your phone number. I told her I'd call you and straighten it out if there was a problem." Did I say too much? I think I did. Looking down at the table, giving thought to what I said... "So obviously you saw her again after that?"

He caught me off guard. I could feel my face turning red. "Yes, I was fishing off the jetty at Holyoke Avenue when she was walking the beach and saw me. She said she saw the article in the paper I wrote and asked if there was any more information about the body I found. She seemed very upset that day, and I wondered why. When I asked what was wrong, she told me you two had an argument over me being at the house."

I didn't want to say too much more for Veronica's sake, not wanting to divulge everything she confided in me. I didn't want him to think I was getting too personally involved.

The whole time we sat there, I was looking across the table with the thought running through my mind. I'm sitting across from a person I think is a serial killer, and maybe his next victim would be someone I've grown attached to__ Very much attached to. I thought, "Yes, Joel, you ass- your wife."

After our beers came to the table, he took out his wallet and paid for the drinks. Looking up at the waitress, he laid down a generous tip. She smiled, thanking him then walked away.

I wanted to pay full attention to what he had to say and I waited. A few seconds passed, he didn't speak... A few more seconds of silence passed, still nothing. He was focused on his glass of beer and began to run his finger over the condensation building up, watching the drops run down to the coaster under his glass.

It seemed like an hour, and I was beginning to get impatient for this conversation to begin- like a pregnant pause in literature when neither person knows exactly what to say, or when to speak.

Slowly looking up at me he finally asked, motioning with his eyes around the room, "Is this where you met Veronica? I know she comes here sometime?"

"No, I never saw her until we met that day at Long Beach Island."

"She did tell me you're the one who found the body on the beach. How's Veronica involved?"

"She's not. Like I said, she only let me use the phone to call the police and watch my dog until I was finished."

"I knew there must have been a dog there. I found an old hair brush of Veronica's on the deck with white dog hair on it."

Pausing for a moment, I thought he was a little strange about scrutinizing everything around him, remembering Veronica telling me he constantly had to have everything showroom perfect. He must be a bitch to live with. I began to understand why she was on edge constantly.

Just as I was going to speak, he interrupted. He seemed very nervous about whether he should ask me the next question, and when he said it, I was completely shocked.

"I'd appreciate it if you didn't try calling my wife."

Feeling uncomfortable with his remark, I adjusted myself in the booth, not knowing how much he knew about our meetings. I decided the best way to deal with him was to say as little as possible.

"How did you know I did, and how did you get my phone number?"

"Simple, when I got home the other day, I picked up the phone and dialed star 11."

I already knew that star 11 redials the last phone number that's been called from a phone. All he had to do was listen to my answering machine to know who I was. The message on my machine would give him my name. It's in the greeting that's announced before asking to leave a recall number.

I thought as Veronica suspected, it was more control. She knew he was jealous, but I don't think she knew the extent of his paranoia. I realized why their marriage was a total disaster. He had to know everything she did when they weren't in each other's company. Was it because of his advanced age or lack of self esteem with a sexual deficiency? From what I experienced in the parking lot at Claxton's, it sure wouldn't appear to be a problem on her part. I wondered if he knew about that too.

Just as that thought passed my mind, it was as though I telegraphed a message to his brain. "How many times have you met her after your first two accidental encounters?

Did he know I took her to the police station on the island? Although, I felt I shook any tail he may have had following her. Did whoever it was have a hunch we may have gone to Long Beach Island and instinctively headed there? If I was writing a story that would be a logical thought. Did they drive by the parking lot at the Town Hall? It's right on the main road. I was almost positive he knew my car, and probably also knew I met her at Lord's and Logan's.

I wanted to know what other deep dark secrets Joel harbored, so I let him talk. The more I knew about their relationship, the better understanding I would have of his dark side, and the more I could relay to Veronica. I felt an urgency to warn her of how much danger she was really facing. It was beginning to look like he was planning to end his relationship with his wife, as he did with his secretaries, and didn't want to take a chance on me interfering.

I commented, "I only met her twice. Once at your house- And the encounter on the beach." I lied. Did he all of a sudden know it? An expression of doubt came over his face, and he became restless in his seat. I felt the red coming to my face and tried to mask it with another lie to protect Veronica. "There's no need for you to fear me taking Veronica away from you, if that's what you're thinking." Although in my mind, that's exactly, what I desperately wanted to do. This conversation had all the earmarks of a joust. I was parrying his questions with innuendo's and outright lies. He looked down at the table, running his finger around the rim of his now empty glass- then slowly looked up wanting to capture my facial reaction to his next question. He sent another shock wave, something I didn't expect.

"Would you accompany me to my apartment? It's close by. I stay there on occasion. I want to show you a report from having her followed, and what your opinion would be?"

It was strange enough that someone who suspects me of seeing his wife would think I'd be interested in anything someone put in a report. I wanted to read just how much of a file he had on her and what it might have in the report about us being together.

Is he trying to show me documentation that I was lying about the two encounters? What if it did? What's my response going to be? I couldn't say the report was wrong. I know too many private investigators.

I have done some following myself with some of the news stories I did. Generally private investigator's reports are accurate- iron clad accurate. Hesitating for a few seconds, then replied, "Yes I would."

I had my derringer in my pocket and remembered Ben mentioning the forensic report, that the victims had chloral hydrate in their system. So I knew not to accept a drink, if, in fact, one was offered.

His apartment was a few blocks away- an eight story- building prominently standing just off City Line Avenue. I was aware of the building as anyone would be. It stood out with its large red neon sign atop the building that proclaimed... Adam's Tower Apartment Building. A relatively new building, the two lower floors comprised the headquarters of Sun Oil Company. The next two floors were occupied by attorney's offices and a few noted physicians and one psychiatrist. The upper floors were apartments.

Driving to the front of the building we were greeted by a doorman dressed in a red jacket with a matching cap. When he opened the car door he commented, "Good evening Mr. Simmons! I didn't recognize the car."

"Howard, it's a lease automobile for the office. Do you have another parking spot for me?"

"I'll make sure I find one." He motioned to a valet.

A young man promptly approached the car, going to the driver's side getting in after we exited the car.

The building with all the attention by the staff, spelled nothing but expensive. Going inside, the information and security desk in the lobby, was staffed 24/7 by two people. One appeared to be a receptionist and the other a security guard. The plush gray carpeting and polished brass would make any building in the area look pale by comparison.

Waiting for the elevator, I looked at the marquis' the titles were impressive. I looked at the psychiatrist's name: M. Silverstein- MD, PHD. LCSW MFT: it read like an eye chart. Thinking to myself, "Sounds expensive. I wonder if he knows he has a potential client living above his office."

The elevator doors opened and the attendant promptly announced, "Good evening Mr. Simmons, a little chilly this evening."

"Good evening Simon ...Yes, it is!"

Stepping into the elevator, the attendant pushed the button for the seventh floor. Exiting the elevator, we proceeded down the hall to his apartment.

Passing the large windows in the corridor, I couldn't help but taking in the breathtaking lighted panoramic view of the city. The building was strategically placed to get the maximum advantage for people who would occupy it at an elaborate cost.

When we got to room 712, Joel took the key from his pocket, and unlocked the door. When we walked in, the first thing I noticed other than the nice furniture, were all the used glasses on the end tables, cigarette butts in the ash trays and the newspaper on the floor- very different from the neatness of the shore house.

Scanning the spacious room, I spied something on a shelf. I thought, "What's that, a statue?" Suddenly, I realized it wasn't. It just moved. A Seale Gray Siamese cat was perched on top of a high shelf over the T.V. He was examining me- a stranger who just entered his domain. I thought, "Where's all the dislike for animals that would mess up a place?"

I sat down on the posh living room sofa, and with ease, the cat leapt off the shelf. Curious of the new invader, it cautiously walked over to me, and with the same ease coming down from the shelf, leapt in my lap. Surprised at his boldness, I sat back.

"That's my companion, Solomon. He can't resist exploring new visitors. You aren't allergic to cats, are you?"

"No, I don't mind cats, but I prefer dogs. They seem more attached, where cats can sometime be standoffish."

"I know what you mean. Solomon sometimes has his moods."

"When I first walked in, I thought the cat was a statue on the shelf until it moved."

"It's funny. It must be instinctive. For some reason Siamese cats seem to like high places. It must be a security thing."

Scanning the room I noticed there were several paintings hanging on the walls that looked like they might be originals. I noticed one in particular. It looked like a Picasso. I moved Solomon to get up and get a closer look.

"Is this an original?"

"Yes, I bought it several years ago at an auction in England. It was advertised by Christie's Auction House in South Kensington. I was there on a trip, and I like his style of painting so I bought it. My wife was with me on that trip."

Temporarily taken by all the elegance, I almost forgot the real reason I was invited there. I thought, "People who have money can afford such luxuries, and the wealthy generally impress the less fortunate, like me."

"Joel you have a beautiful apartment. It's very impressive."

From the moment we walked in, I would glance at him from time to time. He seemed to be following me with his eyes as I explored the paintings, and somehow I got the feeling he didn't really want to be an adversary- Like two animals in the wild getting ready to face off against one another- then suddenly realize they didn't need to.

He had more of a look like, "What will my response be with what he was about to show me?" A look of being half confident that what he had to show me would make the slightest difference in my opinion of him or the outcome of this meeting.

Standing behind a beautiful dark walnut bar in a corner of the room mixing a drink, he looked up.

"Thanks for the compliment. I keep this apartment so I can be myself and don't have to worry about the place always having to look showroom perfect. I can come here and work relaxed if I don't feel like running to Center City."

Something funny struck me. Strange- Those were the exact words Veronica used to describe him.

I asked, "Does your wife live here too?"

"No, it could never look like this if she did. This is my safe haven. We all have to have a place to escape to." Motioning with his hand, "Well, this is mine. Would you care for a drink?"

I thought… "Here it comes, the chloral hydrate drink. No thanks, if you have a beer, I'd appreciate one."

Reaching down, he took a cold beer from the refrigerator under the bar. Holding it above the counter, he opened it. The sound of the pressure escaping the can, reassured me it was safe to drink.

"Care for a glass."

"No thanks!" Thinking, I didn't want to give him the opportunity to put something in it.

My mind was trying to piece this weird scene together. He calls me to meet him- a person who he suspects of making secret rendezvous with his wife, and instead of being hostile; he's polite and offers me a drink. This scenario was beginning to appear like an Alfred Hitchcock movie.

"Look Joel, thanks for the hospitality, but I didn't come up here to be entertained. What is it you wanted to show me?"

Looking up at me, he paused for a few moments; then put down his drink. Stepping out from behind the bar, he went to a nearby cabinet. Taking a key from his pocket, he unlocked the door and retrieved a brown office- type folder. Laying it down on the glass coffee table in front of me as though it was a challenge… like I dare you to have the same opinion of Veronica after you read this.

As I opened the folder to retrieve the contents, a stack of 12 or 15 photos bound together with a rubber band fell to the floor.

Picking them up, I immediately recognized the top photo. It was a close-up of the back of my car and the license plate. It appeared by the background that it was taken at the mall. Unbinding the rubber band holding them together- I noticed another photo- a picture of my car in front of the police station in Beach Haven. Were they placed on top to grab my attention immediately?

By the look on Joel's face, I could tell my assumption was correct. A smirk crossed his face- a real I got you moment. I felt uncomfortable knowing he now knew I was lying. What else did he have recorded on the pages I was about to read? Were there photographs of Veronica and me in the parking lot at Claxton's?

Although it was difficult, I tried to maintain an attitude of being nonchalant. Thumbing through them, I couldn't identify the men and scenes in the next several photos. They meant nothing to me.

Getting to the end of the stack, I saw another photo- a photo that made me stop and look at Joel. To my surprise, instead of an I got you in a lie look, he seemed to have a look of remorse, and it suddenly made me feel small and cheap. It was a photo of Veronica and me leaving Claxon's. I began reading the contents of the folder, and it didn't leave out much. The man entering the car next to mine in the parking lot was the private investigator. Her every move seemed to have been recorded in the report: our meeting at the mall on both occasions and how long we were together.

My- losing the investigator in traffic the morning I drove her to the police station and his intuition of us going to the island was spot on. The wording began to read as if he was going there to possibly get a picture of us going into or leaving the shore house. It said he accidently saw my car at the police station, and continued the surveillance after we left, following us to Claxton's. I continued to read the report, which was quite lengthy, and noticed a few referrals to Veronica having additional affairs, but dismissed them as attempting to be slanderous to her character.

Knowing approximately where I was in the report, he would occasionally glance at me from time to time as I was reading, seemingly expecting a response. After I finished, I laid it down on the coffee table. Looking at him, I couldn't deny it, I confessed my association.

"I won't- or rather can't deny it, I've seen her several times. This is quite a dossier. It must have cost you a pretty penny to have someone report all this. It appears to go back a few years though. Who are the other people?"

"Do you see the picture of the Jaguar?"

"Yes; why?"

"Don't you recognize it?"

"No, how could I know who owns it!"

"It belonged to Howard Krass!"

"Howard Krass?"

"Yes, the same person you did the corruption story on. The same person I told you was a former client."

"I never saw that car before. As far as I knew, he drove a maroon colored Lincoln."

"I've seen that car too. He drove it to the shore house on several occasions. I entertained him and a few of his associates before I decided to drop him as a client."

His words had a stinging affect on my ears. It was beginning to piece together- that Veronica was lying, telling me she didn't know anything about Joel's business. This would certainly undermine some of the things she told me, but how much was a lie? It was beginning to make sense. She must have started the relationship while Joel was entertaining him and his friends.

"To answer your first question Ron- Yes, private detectives don't come cheap. The second is a concern for a wife who might be heading for trouble. As you mentioned, it didn't begin recently."

"What do you mean trouble, like physical trouble?"

"Yes, she's been trying to cover some bruises on her neck. When I asked about them, she blew my question off and didn't give me an answer. I don't know if she said anything to you, but we're in a really difficult time in our marriage.

We'll probably wind up in a divorce, at least that appears to be the case at this point, but I still don't want any harm to come to her."

Snapping back in a defensive tone, "If you think I would abuse any woman, you're insane."

Thinking he may have over stepped his bounds, he said … "No. as I said, I'm just concerned for her welfare."

Bewildered by his statement, I got up and headed for the door. Being embarrassed by the report, my only defense was to leave.

"Goodnight for now, Joel."

"Look Ron. I'm sorry if I offended you, but I think after reading that, you can understand my concern. Are you still going to try seeing her again?"

I noticed his fist was clenched and I sensed it wasn't to be hostile, but rather anxiously wanted to hear me say no. I didn't disappoint him...

"No Joel." I lied again. He unclenched his fist, seemingly relieved at my answer. Why he would suddenly believe me, I couldn't understand. I believe it was his overwhelming desire for a positive answer.

"Thanks for coming!"

On the way down in the elevator and on the drive home, I wondered. Why is he telling me all this? Suddenly, a terrifying thought crossed my mind. Is he trying to convince me that he's not the one responsible for her bruises? Does he think if- or possibly when- she shows up dead, I can be a witness in his defense? Did he want me to think he made the report out of genuine concern for her? All this was being tossed around in my mind as I headed back to my apartment.

Suddenly I pulled to the curb. I couldn't wait until tomorrow to contact Veronica. I felt the urgency to call her now. Knowing Joel was still at his apartment, I tried calling Veronica's home. There was no answer.

I called almost every 15 minutes- then hung up before the answering machine kicked in.

I rushed home, took Daisy for her usual walk- then set out for the island. From the time I left the apartment, subconsciously, I kept looking over my shoulder, making sure I wasn't being followed. Was I getting paranoid after meeting Joel?

I slowly drove by the house and saw the lights on with her car parked in the driveway and another I didn't recognize. Was it Joel's? It wasn't the car we went to his apartment in. The doorman did say he didn't recognize the one he was driving. Was this his personal car that he wasn't using- the one in the parking garage? Did he hurriedly come directly to the shore after our meeting thinking I would come here? I hoped my suspicions about why he wanted me to read the report, weren't going to take place.

Should I confront them both together- and warn her of the report he had? No, that may only inflame a bad situation.

It was a cold night, and I could see smoke coming from the fire-place chimney. It was around 10:30, and I thought it would be kind of useless to think she would be walking the beach on such a cold night.

I parked two blocks away and took Daisy over the walkway to the beach. Unhooking her leash- she burst into a much needed run. Taking her for walks in the city, were pretty much just for constitutional pur-poses. Now that she wasn't restrained, she had a chance to run, and took full advantage of it.

Pulling the collar of my coat up tight to my neck, I braced against the cold, walking toward the firmer surface of the sand. As adamant as I was about seeing her, being so cold after an hour walking the beach, it finally got to me, and I retreated to the car. I think Daisy was just as glad. After drying her, she didn't need coaxing, and leapt into the passenger seat. Still shivering from being cold, she lay down on the seat beside me and sighed. As I slowly drove by Veronica's house again, Joel's car was gone and only Veronica's car remained.

Thinking to myself- shall I? Why not? I parked several houses away, not wanting to take a chance on being seen, then knocked on the door.

Opening it, she stepped back surprised to see me.

"Ron, what on earth are you doing here? Don't tell me you were walking the beach with Daisy as cold as it is? Come on in and get warm." She put her hands over my ears. "Your ears are freezing and red from the cold."

The warmth from her hands felt good, and I was glad I made the decision to knock. She sat in the corner of the couch in the fetal position, holding a pillow in front of her. I sat on the sofa on the other side of the glass coffee table, opposite her.

"When I drove by a while ago there were two cars here. Was that Joel's car?"

She hesitated. "Yes, it was Joel. I didn't know why he drove all the way to the shore to scream at me. He just left in a rage."

Putting two and two together, I was right. It was Joel's car. He must have come here directly after our meeting. The fireplace was glowing and I could feel the warmth from it. I envisioned being offered a drink and sitting down with her to tell her about my meeting with Joel, but the offer never came forward.

"Veronica, I got a surprise phone call tonight. You'll never guess who it was."

"Who was it, another phone call from the police? Is that why you're down here?" She looked at me waiting for an answer.

"No, it wasn't the police. It was from Joel. He wanted to meet me at the sports bar on City Line Avenue."

Looking puzzled, she stared at me for a few moments, absorbing my words. "Joel? You're kidding me. How the hell did he get your phone number?"

"At first I wondered the same thing. I thought he may have seen my phone number I wrote for you, but I was wrong. He told me when he gets home he always goes to the telephone and dials star 11."

"Why, what can he learn from that?"

"That automatically redials the last call made from that phone. All he had to do was listen to my answering machine to find out my name.

From now on, whoever you call, make sure the last call is erased. Even if you dial a partial number then hang up. All it will do is redial that partial number. Either that, or call a friend just to say hello."

"That's something. I never knew that. That must be why__"

She abruptly stopped... "Why, what?"

"Never mind... Did you meet with him? What did he have to say?"

"Yes, I met him at the sports bar on City Line Avenue. He asked if that's where I met you. He said you go there sometimes. The first thing he said was... 'I'd appreciate it if you would stop seeing my wife.' ...I know you don't realize it, but he has quite a dossier on you. It must be twenty pages thick. There's even a mention of our meetings at the mall on both occasions. He also has a stack of about twenty photos."

"That bastard... Photo's of what?"

"Picture's of you with different people. One of the pictures is us coming out of the Town Hall in Beach Haven and another of us at Claxton's. There were also a few pictures of the back of cars with the license numbers, mine is among them."

She paused for a moment then said... "Do you remember the make or model of the cars?"

"Only one stood out in my mind. It was a Jaguar, a gray Jaguar. Do you happen to know who owns that?"

I noticed she purposely looked away from me, not wanting to make eye contact. Not knowing how much Joel told me, she replied. "That was one of Joel's clients, but that was two years ago. He picked me up at the house on a few occasions and drove me to the shore. Joel would come down later, and we would drive home together rather than take two cars."

"I saw several different men in other pictures, but I don't remember what they looked like."

Her face became red with anger, and she threw the small cushion from the sofa she was holding across the room. Jumping up from the sofa she said. "I can't believe it! I can't believe it! That sneaky bastard! No wonder he drove all the way down here. I was surprised when he came in yelling. I wondered what the hell it was all about."

"I thought that might have been his car when I drove by earlier, that's why I didn't stop. To tell you the truth, when I saw it, I was afraid he might have come down to murder you."

She shook her head then turned away from me, very disturbed. Taking another plush pillow from the end of the sofa, she punched it- then threw it across the room. When she turned in my direction, I immediately noticed she was wringing her hands- the same way she did standing next to the car, the day I gave her my phone number.

She said... "That's the last straw. I'm not going to put up with his shit any longer."

I've never seen her angry, and it disturbed me. I told her again. "Don't do anything foolish. Be careful about dealing with him. I told you before, if you need a place to stay, my door's always open."

I was kind of happy to hear that she finally came to her senses, and I thought my chances with her were looking a little better. I was glad I made the trip. Walking to the door, she opened it. "Ron, you better go. I want time to think things over."

"What's there to think over? If this doesn't convince you to get the hell away from him now, nothing will. He's dangerous. As I was reading the report, I wondered if he was just building a case of infidelity against you. Then something else crossed my mind. Was he showing me that to make me think he's genuinely concerned? Maybe he's showing me all this- just letting me know if you wind up missing or dead. By his report, that I'll be implicated. Maybe he thinks he could be able to put pressure on me to the point where he needs a character witness."

"Oh, after what you just told me, I'm definitely leaving him. I want out- out!"

I was disappointed that I wasn't invited to stay longer and possibly have a drink, but seeing how angry and frustrated she was, I didn't want to press the issue. She opened the door and a sudden draft of cold air rushed in.

Pulling her robe closed around her neck, she remarked. "Boy its cold- I hate to see winter coming." Looking out at the darkness of the cold night she shivered. "Goodnight Ron." ...After giving me a light peck on the lips, she closed the door behind me. On the way back to the city, I was glad she finally made up her mind to leave and felt good about my chances with her, might be a little better.

Several days had passed since I last spoke to her, and I was beginning to worry again. I thought about what she told me the night I made the surprise visit after the meeting with her husband. I remember her saying that, she wondered why Joel drove all the way to the shore just to scream and yell at her. I wondered if she was alright, and if she was still having problems, why hasn't she called?

There wasn't any need to go to the island without meeting her, and not wanting to go to her house in the city, I was at a dead end.

As each day that passed without hearing a word from her, I was beginning to fear the worst. I traveled to the island twice within the week but failed to see her car, or any car for that matter. I was worried enough that I considered going to Joel's apartment and getting physical with him. He must have seen her, or at least knows where she's at and how she's doing. I decided against it, just in case she already left him and was trying to set herself up in a new life away from his abuse. I got back into the grind of working and back to the hum drum of boredom, but my mind was still constantly on her. Everything else seemed secondary.

It's when you least expect something is when it usually happens. I returned from work a week after I last saw her, and there was a message on my answering machine. The phone number was different than the one she gave me previously and I anxiously returned her call. I was hoping she was finally separated and in her own apartment looking forward to a new life, possibly with me.

"Can we meet some place? I want to fill you in on what's happening with Joel."

"Are you in your own place? I'll come there."

"No, I'm at my friend's right now. Can we meet at that same restaurant we were in before- the one at the mall?"

"I'll be there in about an hour."

Anxious as an expectant father, I wove in and out of traffic on the expressway, trying to get there as fast as I could, without getting pulled over by the police for speeding. When I pulled into the mall parking lot, I found an empty parking space near the entrance. To my surprise, she exited the front entrance as soon as she saw my car, hurriedly walking across the lot. I reached across to the passenger door handle and let her in.

"I thought we were supposed to meet in the restaurant?"

"Not now. Now that I know I'm constantly being followed."

I snapped at her in an annoyed tone... "Where the hell have you been? I've been going out of my mind with worry. Why haven't you called?"

"After your surprise encounter with Joel, I don't want to cause you anymore problems."

"Look, I'm not afraid for myself. I'm afraid for you."

"Listen Ron, Joel's been going to the shore house with his new secretary. I'm afraid he's setting her up as his next victim. I just wanted to reassure you that you're not out of my life. I don't want you to be angry with me, just be patient."

"I will, but don't keep me worrying- at least leave a message."

"I promise I won't do that again."

She leaned over and kissed me. I asked, "Where's Joel now?"

"He told me he's spending long hours at work, but I think he knew I didn't believe him. That's why I'm with a friend."

I never asked her where his office was in the city, so I thought now may be a good time to ask. "Exactly where is his office?"

"He brokers from his office on Chestnut Street or an apartment he has, just off City Line Avenue."

"You mean the Adam's Tower Apartment Building?"

She looked surprised... "How did you know that?"

"Remember, you mentioned it once. I never thought to tell you, but we only met at the Sports Bar. I looked at the folder in his apartment?"

Why did you want to meet this evening? Was it just to let me know about him going to the shore house with his secretary?" Sarcastically I added, "Or did you want me to know that you were still alive?"

"You know I care about you, and I love the concern you have for me. I assure you it works both ways lover."

She directed me to let her out at the end of the employee parking lot where her car was parked. Before getting out, she leaned over and gave me a kiss. As I watched her getting into her car, I was glad she finally called and we were able to meet.

Even though it's an hours drive, I was content that she was ok, and finally decided to stay with a friend. It took a lot of worry off my mind.

On the drive home, I let my mind fantasize. I thought about my own lifestyle, then suddenly realized. She would be taking a step down to be attached to someone like me- a long step down. She was Mercedes Benz or better, and I was Chevy- strictly Chevy, with no illusions of anything better.

There have been stranger things happen to people of prominence. Men married to wealthy women- running off with their tennis teacher- and wealthy women leaving everything behind to run off with the chauffer. At least I had a better chance financially than either one of them.

Chapter 6

The next few days went by without a word from her. Is she pulling this shit again, I thought what is it with her? It's like she gets some sort of twisted enjoyment out of seeing me worry. I made up my mind that it wasn't going to happen again. She was either going to resolve her situation, or I'm history. I'll just have to turn mother's picture to the wall, as the saying goes, and walk away.

It was easy to think, but somehow my anger wasn't walking in step with my feelings, and I began to question my anger. She did say she was interested. That's a positive. After work one day this week, I'll test the water and see just how deep her feelings really are by paying her a surprise visit.

The anxiety was still ever present in my mind, and within two days, my intention became reality and I made the trip.

As I slowly passed Veronica's, I strained to see if her car was parked in the driveway. There was another car; one I never saw before- an older Chevy. I assumed with that car being there, maybe Joel's car is in the garage and the Chevy may have been his secretary's, the one Veronica was worried about.

Was it? Maybe it is. I parked two blocks away, and went over the walkway to the beach. It was a clear, cold blustery night, with a strong wind blowing straight down the beach. Occasionally, a gust of wind would blow the sand up into swirls around my face and force me to stop, turning my back against the wind. Bracing against the cold, I pulled my coat collar up tight to my neck, continuing to Veronica's. Was I foolish to think I was going through all this for nothing? I didn't know, but something was driving me on. Would I see Joel come out of the house with his secretary? Should I just jot down the license number and give it to Veronica, so she can use it against him when she files for a divorce? Is this the night Veronica was suspicious of? Is he going to commit a murder as she mentioned? Thinking she may be right, I pressed on.

As I crested the rise of the walkway near her house, I looked up at the picture window. I could see what appeared to be two people silhouetted behind the closed drapes, perhaps a man and a woman.

I looked in horror as the man seemed to strike the woman, then grab her by the neck. Her arms began thrashing- punching back, trying to escape the strangle hold. Then suddenly the lighting in the room changed. It looked like a lamp was either knocked over- or turned off, and the silhouettes became less distinguishable. Even with the loss of light, I could still see her arms were thrashing. It looked as if she was slowly losing strength, diminishing her resistance to his assault. Her arms slowly dropped to her sides, and I realized at that point, she was probably dead. It all happened so quickly. Did I witness something that was real, or was it something I was imagining?

With the history of events since mid- September, I wasn't quite sure. No, it couldn't have been my imagination. Just as Veronica feared, I just witnessed Joel murdering his secretary. In a state of panic, not knowing what I was going to witness next, I wondered if I should knock at the door and completely surprise him. Or should I just hurry to the police station and tell them what I just witnessed? I thought that would certainly be the end Veronica's troubles.

Witnessing the event seemed to put my mind on high alert. I didn't think he'd want to keep the body there very long, and I realized his car must be in the garage. Knowing he would have to emerge with it soon, I hid on a deck two houses away. I wanted to position myself where I could keep his car and the window in full view. From here, I could also see the doorway leading into the garage and the door leading down the stairs to the driveway, not knowing exactly which way he would come out. I could still see the man's silhouette moving back and forth behind the drapes and waited to see what was going to happen.

In a few minutes, just as I thought, the door opened. I was right. He's coming out. With the light shining behind the man, I really couldn't get a good look at his face.

Stepping out the door, he slowly scanned the area, then, walked to the Chevy, opening the trunk. He went back in the garage and retrieved what appeared to be a shovel. After placing it in the trunk, he returned to the house. In a few minutes, he came out again with what looked like a body slung over his shoulder. It was wrapped in a blanket, and as I watched, I cataloged to memory his every move. He walked over to the car looking cautiously around. He struggled trying to put the body in the trunk when the blanket unwrapped, falling to the ground.

Yes, I could see it a little plainer. It was a body- a dead body. What appeared to be a lifeless young person whose life had just been snuffed out by a perverted person- a man without a shred of feeling or remorse.

This would make the fourth body, and his movements indicated to me, it was well choreographed and he had it down to a science. It appeared the woman was tall with long hair. But wait, is she naked? I wished the lighting was a little better. Did his perversions extend to him keeping underwear of his victims for some weird fantasy?

I've investigated stories like this before, where the murderer some-times had such motives. That's probably what it is. Veronica did say she found a pair of underwear in the trunk of his car.

Watching him closely, he hurriedly picked up the blanket and care-fully covered the body, tucking it around her as if he was sheltering her from the cold- Then closed the trunk.

A cold ending... not like a normal funeral with pomp and circum-stance, or even the privilege of a casket. Only a temporary sepulcher she shared, with probably a car jack, a spare tire and a shovel.

Looking around again to make sure he wasn't seen, he quietly pushed down on the trunk to ensure it was closed- then returned to the house.

Do I make a break and get to the police station, so they can catch him here? No, I'd be better off waiting. He has to get rid of the car with the body. It can't be very far. It'll have to be within walking distance. He has to return for his own car if it's in the garage. I was right in my assumption. A few minutes later he exited again, unlocking the car door, then got in. He didn't wait for the engine to warm. He put it in gear immediately then slowly drove down the street, without turning on the headlights. At the end of the block, he turned them on- then made a right turn. My heart was racing so fast. I didn't feel the cold any longer. Still not knowing whether to go to the police immediately, or watch to see if he would return, I waited.

Suddenly something caught my eye. It can't be- someone's still in the house. Wait a minute. There it is again. It passed in front of the drapes. Wait. There it is again. There's another person walking around the room.

Is that a woman? Yes, there it is again. It's definitely a woman. I suddenly realized there weren't just two people in the house; there were three.

If that's the case, who's was the girl in the trunk? It couldn't have been Veronica. The girl being carried was too big. Was this another one of Joel's fantasies? He and another woman having some twisted fantasy with the enjoyment of killing someone? I wondered what kind of macabre scene I just witnessed.

A chilling thought ran through my mind. Would Veronica's life end the same way- cold blooded and heartless? Will the woman I began to fall in love with meet the same cold ending?

Still focused on the drapes, it looked like a woman trying to straighten up. Yes, it is. The lighting became brighter. She must have just put the lamp back in place.

In about ten minutes, a car came down the street in my direction. I quickly ducked down behind a neighbor's steps to avoid being seen by the oncoming headlights. Did they catch a glimpse of me? I didn't know. Suddenly, the car pulled into a driveway several houses from the beach then turned out the headlights. That must be someone who lives there. I felt relieved. Should I make a break for it now and head for the police station?

Just as I was getting up, I quickly ducked down again. Another car entered the street, and I waited to see where it would go. To my surprise, it pulled into Veronica's driveway. It was a Lincoln and not the Chevy that left. Was it a different person coming to the house just for a visit? Why couldn't they have gotten here a little sooner, so they could have witnessed something as shocking as I had.

Wait a minute- That's the same car I saw the night I came to tell Veronica about the meeting with Joel. It's his. After he got out of the car, I could see it was Joel. He must have had his car parked somewhere close by, where he intended to dump the body. This thing had to be well planned- premeditated as you can get. After he exited the car, I could see it was the same person who left- The same figure of the man who put the body in the trunk. On second thought, it's not the same figure I saw when I met Joel.

This man carried that body with ease and was a lot stockier. Is Joel still in the house too? That's his car. Could there have been four people in the house? This person: the woman whose shadow was on the drapes, and Joel. Is this some sort of sacrificial cult? Was Joel still in there? I watched until he entered the house then ran back to where I parked, two blocks away.

The run down the beach seemed a lot shorter with the wind blowing sand at my back, not in my face. At this point my numbness wasn't from the cold. It was from what I just witnessed. The desire to get to the police station before anyone left the house was foremost in my mind. I felt like a kid again in the middle of a nightmare, trying to get away from an imaginary creature, but my legs just wouldn't move fast enough. There was one distinct difference. This was real- very real.

Getting to the car, I fumbled with the keys, dropping them in the sand. With the aid of the street light, I finally found them. Wiping the sand off, I finally got the door open. I started the engine and stepped on the gas pedal. The engine raced before I realized I was still in park. Throwing the gear shift in reverse, I backed all the way down the street without turning on the headlights.

Could it have been Joel- this third person- and his secretary killing someone? Every scenario was possible, and in the short drive to the police station, I thought of at least 10. It all boiled down to the fact that I just saw someone killed, and I was certain there was someone else in the house when it took place.

I pulled up in front of the town hall and saw the lights on at the police department office. Turning off the motor, I hurried up the stairs of the building, throwing open the door. I looked down the dimly lit hall and all the offices were closed for the exception of the police department. The light shining through the glass window was like a beacon of safety. Like the safe feeling from that bad dream, waking up to find yourself in the comfort of your own bed.

I franticly ran down the hall and knocked at the police department door. I didn't realize how hard I knocked, but it left no doubt to whomever was inside, that I wanted immediate attention because I had an emergency.

A man's voice from behind the door bellowed. "Whoever it is, don't break the damn glass. Come in!"

Entering the room, Ben looked up from his typewriter. Seeing I was upset, he quickly got up from his chair.

"What gives Ron- you trying to break the damn glass? You look a little shaken. What's the problem?"

"Ben, I've just seen someone being murdered!"

His eyes focused on me, trying to comprehend what I just said.

Realizing I was serious, he quickly walked over to where his jacket was hanging, focusing on me the whole time.

"Where did you witness this?"

"At Veronica's- the woman you interviewed."

"Was it her?"

"It didn't look like her. All I saw, was the silhouettes of what looked like a man strangling a woman, then carry a limp body wrapped in a blanket out of the house and put it in the trunk of a car."

"Are they still there?"

"They were a few minutes ago. I got here as fast as I could."

"Come on. Show me where it happened."

I followed as he hurriedly exited the room. After getting in his patrol car, we started for the house. As I continued telling him what I witnessed, he picked up his car microphone and radioed to another police car.

"Kevin, this is Ben. Meet me at the main road and Troy Avenue- the dead end street where the Simmons house is. Where are you now?"

"I'm at the far end of the township checking the lumber yard. Why, what's happening?"

"I'll explain it when we meet."

We were at the rendezvous before the other patrol car and waited for a few minutes, and got out of the vehicle as Kevin approached.

"You remember Ron? He's the one who found the body on the beach a few months ago."

"Yes, I remember."

"Ron said he witnessed a murder in the second house down the beach at the Simmons' home."

"How did he witness that?"

"I was walking the beach and saw the silhouettes through the drapes."

Zipping up his jacket as he shivered, Kevin replied, "You just happen to be walking the beach on a night like this?"

"No, it was my intention to go there. When I saw an older Chevy, I thought maybe her husband Joel was there with his secretary and his car may have been in the garage. I decided not to knock."

"Tell me again Ron. Are you sure what you're telling me is correct?"

"Yes, Ben, I witnessed the whole thing from the beach. The people were silhouetted through the closed drapes. It looked like the man hit the woman on the head with something- I think it was a lamp. It looked like he strangled her until she went limp. I hid on the deck of the house next door, waiting to see what would happen. About 10 minutes later, he carried out a body. He put it in the trunk of the Chevy that was parked there then drove away. He returned in that Lincoln about 15 minutes later- the one that's in the driveway now. It's Joel's, Veronica's husband."

"Kevin, that looks like Carl Dunn's car."

"Yea Ben, I was thinking the same thing. I'd know that car anywhere."

"Ron, were you on the beach the whole time?"

"No." I pointed to where I was hiding. "I was over there. I hid behind the steps on the neighbor's patio where I could watch the front door."

"Tell us what happened then?"

"I think it must have been a lamp that he hit her with, or it was knocked over in the struggle. The room became darker, but I could still see the shadows. I was shocked when I saw someone else in the house."

"Who did you see?"

"I can't say for sure. The shadow moved across the window very fast, but it appeared to be a woman."

"Then what happened?"

Kevin listened intently as I explained.

"About 10 minutes after I witnessed the murder, a man came out of the house with the body thrown over his shoulder. It was a woman wrapped in a blanket. She had long hair, and from what I could see, she was naked. He put her in the trunk of an older model Chevy that was parked here then drove away."

Kevin asked, "How did you know she was naked if she was wrapped in a blanket?"

"As he was putting it in the trunk of the car, the blanket fell off, and I could see it was a woman, a young woman."

"I don't want you to think I doubt your word. I just want to make sure before I knock on that door. People of prominence down here can make our life miserable... especially if we're wrong."

Both officers walked over to the Lincoln looking it over, after examining it.

"Yes, Kevin, this is Carl's car."

"Yea, like I said... I'd know this car anywhere."

I remarked, "Come to think about it, Ben, the guy who carried out the body was a lot bigger than Joel. I met Joel in the city. He's tall and thin. This guy was tall but bulkier. I don't think Joel could have carried that body with ease. I remember meeting Carl the day I found the body on the beach. I was about to leave Veronica's when he arrived. His frame would be a lot closer match to the man I saw."

"Let's go Kevin. I don't know who may be in there, so be ready. Ron: just in case, for your own safety- stand behind us."

"Ok, Ben, I don't want to be in the way."

We walked to the door leading to the car port where the person carrying the body came from. I stood behind them when Ben knocked. When the door opened, I was shocked to see Veronica standing there. She didn't see me at first, but when Ben stepped to one side, she noticed, and her face went livid- a completely blank look, an astonished look of surprise. She must have been the form I saw walking around after the man, whoever he was, left with the body. I began to understand why she didn't want to tell Ben more when he interviewed her several months ago.

Ben asked, "Is there anyone else in the house?"

Still looking in disbelief that the police were there, and I obviously had something to do with their presence, her attitude changed from shock, to sounding coy.

"Ron! What a surprise. Are you so worried about me you have to come with an army of police?"

Ben asked again in a sterner voice, "Is there anyone else in the house?"

Just then, the shadow of a man appeared at the top of the stairs. Hesitating, he started down. As he came into view, the look on Ben's face was as if someone had died. A discouraged, frustrating look that anyone could plainly see was something very troubling to him. The man was a long- time trusted friend, a person Ben had known for most of his life. It was Carl Dunn, the contractor who built Veronica's house. The man Veronica introduced me to as a friend.

"Carl, you and Mrs. Simmons have to come to police headquarters. I'd like to talk to you."

"What's this all about Ben?"

"Ron here said he witnessed silhouettes of someone being strangled behind the drapes in the front window. Is there anyone else in the house?"

Carl's head seemed to droop, casting his eyes down at the ground.

"No, Ben, just the two of us."

"Get your coats. You have to come with me to the police station."

We followed them up the stairs to the entry of the living room. As I scanned the room while they were getting their coats, I noticed there were signs of a struggle. Ben went back down the stairs and stepped outside to speak to Kevin. As they were discussing what steps they were going to take with their investigation, I remained at the entrance of the living room. The large dirt spot on the floor could have only come from one place, the large tropical plant at the end of the sofa. Everything else seemed to be in order. The room was exactly as I remember the night I surprised Veronica with my unexpected visit- The same night I was so concerned for her safety, I drove the 65 miles just on a chance I may have been able to see her. The night she told me the car that's in the driveway now was Joel's, when actually it belongs to Carl. The very night I was told to leave because she had some serious thinking to do, about how she was going to leave her husband. The night I hoped we could be together for awhile, but was turned out in the cold instead.

The painting in my mind of Veronica was beginning to look like the picture of Dorian Gray. Like the cover over a portrait being removed, it exposed a decaying, rotten to the core, lying, scheming, sneaky, person.

Yes, the room was exactly the same- showroom perfect- for the exception of the evidence of the struggle.

After returning with their coats- Ben said, "Kevin, take Carl in your vehicle, I'll take Mrs. Simmons in mine."

"Ok, Ben. Carl, come with me!"

Still trying to maintain her innocent composure, Veronica asked, "Ron, why on earth would you be on the beach on a night like this?"

"Is that all you can ask after what I witnessed? It's all done, Veronica-the sweet, poor little help- me attitude has played out."

Ben remarked, "Mrs. Simmons, I have to warn you that anything you say can and will be used against you, if the investigation goes in your direction. Maybe it's best if you didn't talk at all until we're at Headquarters."

Chapter 7

Arriving at the police station, Kevin was already inside with Carl. Entering the office, Ben said, "Ron, I'd like to begin with your statement. Kevin, take Carl in the other room."

"Ok, Ben."

"Ron, from the beginning- Tell me what happened tonight, and not so fast. I'm not that good with a typewriter."

I began to relate my story with Veronica in the room, unfurling the event as they happened. The deeper I got into my interview, the more she was unsettled in her chair, shifting from one side to the other. When I got to the description of what I witnessed at the window, her face became black with anger. It grew blacker with every word of condemnation that was coming from my lips, describing the violence of the shadows on the drapes.

If looks could kill, I know in my mind, given the chance, she would have silenced my testimony. The face I thought was so foreign to the woman I had so quickly put on a pedestal was giving me the look of death. Being in the same room hearing my account of what happened was tearing at her inner soul. She realized, like a snared animal, there wasn't much room for escape. There was no way she could lie her way out of what I was saying. She was trapped in her own little web of deception.

As I continued describing the events of the evening, Ben was typing as fast as he could. Noticing he was falling behind, I paused every now and then for him to catch up.

Glancing at her whenever I did pause, I noted she was sneering at me. Her eye contact was as though she was giving me a look. Yes, given the chance to silence me, I would have been dead- as dead as the girl who was strangled. Something I could have never imagined from a person I was so much in love with only a few short hours ago. In a few minutes, Kevin opened the door from the inner office.

"Ben, sorry to interrupt, but Carl wants to speak to you alone."

Ben rose from his chair to exchange offices with Kevin then closed the door. I looked at Veronica who was now in a state of desperation because of what Carl might be saying. In about five minutes, Ben opened the door.

"Kevin, bring Mrs. Simmons in here to wait. I want to finish Ron's interview, then get a statement from Carl. He decided to give me a full confession."

Veronica, in the exchange of rooms, cursed at Carl as she passed. "You stupid bastard- I should have known better than to trust you."

"Carl, take a seat. I'm going to turn on this tape recorder and record our conversation. Don't pay any attention to her. You realize that anything you say here can and will be held against you in a court of law?"

"Yes, Ben, I understand."

"The first thing I want to know is where did you take the victim tonight?"

"I took her to Jackson and Carson Streets. I buried her in a shallow grave. I left the car parked about a block away."

"Ok, Carl, start at the beginning. When did your relationship with Mrs. Simmons begin?"

"It all started when I was discussing the plans to build their house."

"How long ago was that?"

"Three years ago. In the process of building it, the economy took a nose dive, and most of the building on the island was at a standstill."

"I remember that. Go on!"

"I was stretched pretty tight and didn't have enough funds to finish their house, or the few others I already had going for that matter. I was afraid to lose everything. Veronica realizing the pace of work on her house was slowing- asked why. I couldn't mask my position any longer and finally told her about my predicament. She said she would speak to her husband about financing me until I finished her house. After that Joel and I became partners."

"What do you mean, partners- something officially written by a lawyer?"

"Not really. He had the funds I didn't have. It was around the time of the financial market meltdown in 73, when I couldn't even borrow money. The banks just weren't lending any, and my extra money was already gone. Carla and I had to mortgage our own home and sell the shore house we had just to stay afloat. It was a really bad time. I had several projects already going that had the frame work done, and his to complete. I really didn't have much of a choice."

"What was his interest in the partnership?

"We agreed to a 10 percent share in the profits and a discount on his home. Like I said, I didn't have much of a choice. It was either that or go bankrupt."

"When did the relationship with Veronica become personal?"

"Shortly after he agreed to finance me, I think she had a lot to do with it. She would come down to the construction site asking questions about the house, always finding something that needed my immediate attention. One day she was here and it was near six o'clock. I made a suggestion for her to join me and my wife Carla for dinner."

"Was her husband there?"

"No, he couldn't make it for some reason. I don't recall."

"Sorry for the interruption, go on."

"During the course of dinner, Veronica and Carla seemed to hit it off pretty good. They became friends. A few times Carla made the trip to the city and they went shopping together."

"When did the relationship become intimate?"

"About six months after I finished the house. Things were still a little tight with me and Carla. We were arguing over the business, and when she found out Joel was taking 10 percent of everything, it made her mad."

"Did Carla know there was a relationship between you and Veronica?"

"I don't think so- at least not at first. I remember one day Carla returned from a shopping trip to the city and was pretty pissed off."

"Why?"

"I don't really know. Whatever it was about, she never said. It seemed after that time, she wanted to avoid Veronica's company as much as possible. It could have been over Joel's interest in the business. Maybe they had an argument over that. As I said, I really don't know."

"Knowing you personally, Carl, is that why you and Carla got divorced? Was it because of something Veronica said or did?"

"I don't think so. It seemed as though whatever was said, Carla became more suspicious of my every move. If I was at a job site too long or with a client too long, she wanted to know where I was and what time I left. It became so bad- we began to have arguments over it, and not just Joel's interest in the business."

Ben shook his head in disbelief of Carl's confession and asked, "Carl, for someone as successful as you, how did you ever get involved with something like this?"

Carl cast his eyes down to the floor, too embarrassed to look at Ben or answer his question. Then continued...

"After Carla left me, Veronica would call or come down to the job sites where I was working. She always brought me a cold drink, or if it was lunch time, a sandwich or coffee. I was falling in love with her charm and concern for me, not to mention she's a beautiful woman. She was filling a gap in my life. A hole she actually caused when Carla left- and I knew it was bound to end up only one way- by becoming lovers."

Listening to Carl, I thought to myself, I know the feeling.

"What about your relationship with Joel? Were you still friends or financially connected?"

"Yes, we were still financially connected. Veronica began to over-see the money for different projects I was working on. In fact, she took over Carla's place as bookkeeper. I guess Joel was in his own world at the time."

"You said at that time. Is there something else going on?"

"No, Joel was just under a lot of pressure. His father had just passed away, and he was in the process of getting the business transferred into his name. I remember him telling me he had his work cut out for him, building confidence in some of his father's wealthier clients."

"Did his father's death have anything to do with Veronica?"

"No, I don't think he ever liked her. But no, he was an old man, with plenty of health problems."

"Did Joel suspect you and Veronica were intimate?"

"Shortly after we became partners, Joel questioned me about all the time she was spending at the shore. He bluntly asked one day if I was seeing her."

"Well, were you? What did you say?"

"At the time I wasn't. It took me completely by surprise. It actu-ally shocked me. I never thought he could be harboring those kinds of suspicions. In fact, when he said it, I could feel my own face getting red and I think he noticed. I remember telling him, "If you're accusing me of something I'm not doing, I might just as well do it and wear the label."

"What did he say then?"

"I guess he believed me. He apologized and didn't ask anymore."

"What happened tonight?"

"Ben, I have to begin at the beginning, or this interview wouldn't make any sense. It started about 10 months ago- or maybe a little more- probably closer to a year."

"Let me get one thing straight. Carl, what Ron saw tonight, was it the first murder you were involved in?"

"No__ There's been four all together."

"Then you've been involved in all four?"

"Yes. Well, no. Not in their murders, only disposing of the bodies."

"But you did strangle the girl tonight?"

"Yes, but let me start from the beginning, where I first discovered the change in Veronica and her personality."

"What do you mean- change in her personality?"

Ben and I looked at each other, hanging on- waiting for a confession that would rock this little hamlet to its foundation. After all, four murders. Things like this are only supposed to happen in big cities.

Carl continued. "One night over a year ago, just after Veronica and I became intimate, she called me. She was very upset and sounded like she was crying. At first I thought it might have been about a fight with Joel. She was constantly telling me about her unhappy marriage. She asked me to come right over, that it was important. I never heard her that upset before, so I rushed to the house as fast as I could. She always sounded upset whenever she talked about Joel, so I thought the call that night was all about an argument, about them separating. When she told me to come over, I realized Joel must not have been there. After I got to the house, I knocked, but she didn't answer the door. I began to worry for her safety and used the key I had to get in."

"Why did you have a key?"

"They told me to keep it. I had it from the time I finished the house. If they needed something done when they weren't home, I could let myself in."

"Go on."

"When I walked in that night, she was sitting at the end of the sofa with her hands to her face crying. I asked, 'Where's Joel? Why didn't you answer the door?' She said he was in the city and wouldn't return until the next evening. When I stepped further into the room, I could see a young girl lying on the floor next to the coffee table. She wasn't moving and looked like she was dead."

"How was she dressed?"

She was fully dressed, all except her shoes. There was a pair lying on the floor. I just thought they were hers. Why are you asking?"

"Just something on my mind... Go on. Were you sure the girl was dead?"

"I knelt down next to her and tried to feel for a pulse, but there was none. Yes, she was dead."

"Do you know who the girl was?"

"If I can remember right, I think Veronica said her name was Carmen. I don't remember her last name. She was a Puerto Rican girl who lived in Philadelphia. That's all I remember."

"Go on. Then what happened?"

"I asked who she was and what happened to her."

"She told me it was one of Joel's secretaries. She comes to the shore once in awhile with cocaine, and they'd get high together. Veronica said when she came that night, she was already high, and they did a little more together, and had a few drinks. She told me Carmen sat down at the end of the sofa then just sort of slouched. Veronica said she thought she just fell asleep. When she shook her trying to wake her up, she rolled forward and fell off the sofa. She said she didn't move, and didn't know what to do, so she called me. After I felt for a pulse, Veronica asked if she was dead. When I told her yes, she completely lost it and became hysterical. I had to slap her face to bring her back to her senses. I told her we'd have to call the police, but she insisted on waiting."

"Why did she want to wait?"

"She was afraid if there was a coroner's report, it would implicate her with the use of drugs."

"What did you do then?"

"She asked me to wait until it got dark then help her get rid of the body.   Looking at her in a state of panic, something I wasn't use to, for some stupid reason, I did as she asked."

"Did she suggest how?"

"She asked me to bury her on one of the vacant lots not being built on. She knew I was familiar with most of them and which ones were scheduled for development. We waited until it got dark, then I wrapped her in a blanket and carried her downstairs. Veronica looked to see if there was anyone around and opened the trunk of my car. After I put her in, she rode with me to the vacant lot and was the lookout while I buried her."

"Which lot was that?"

"The one next to George's Bait and Tackle Shop."

"What happened after that?"

"It seemed like after taking the burden off her shoulders, we became even more intimate and were in each other's company as often as we could. The divorce with Carla was taking its toll on me, and I needed an ear to listen to my troubles. Veronica and me- we even discussed getting married after she got her divorce."

"You said that's the one buried next to the bait shop; where were the others buried?"

"Let me finish. About three months later, she called me to the house again. There was another dead girl lying on the floor. I asked who it was, and she told me it was another one of Joel's secretaries. I asked her what happened this time, if they were doing drugs too. She told me No. They just had a few drinks, that's all. Veronica said when she went to the bathroom, the girl looked fine. She thought she might have passed out and hit her head on the end of the coffee table. There was a mark on the side of her temple, so I thought that might have been the case."

"Do you know her name? Was she a person that Veronica did drugs with too?"

"I didn't know the girl or remember her name. I never personally saw Veronica doing drugs, but I know her and Joel's circle of friends did cocaine on occasion."

 "What did you do then?"

"Like the other body, I buried it on another vacant site."

"Who was the girl tonight? Was she a secretary?"

"No, she was blackmailing me and Veronica. She didn't have anything to do with Joel's business."

Ben looked up, surprised at the different direction with the interview… "What do you mean blackmailing you?"

"She saw us burying the body of Karen White on the beach in late September- just before the storm. She contacted Veronica and described our every move that night, so we knew she had to be watching us. She said she followed us back to the house afterward."

"OK, the girl buried on the beach- Why was she killed?"

"Veronica told me Joel asked for a divorce… She suspected him of wanting to marry her."

"Did he ask her for the divorce?"

"Not then. She said they had arguments about it before but not recently. When she found a receipt from a jewelry store in Philadelphia where he purchased an expensive blue sapphire ring, she realized what was going to possibly happen."

When he said blue sapphire ring- Ben and I looked at each other.

"I told Veronica, 'Why not give it to him! Wouldn't that be good for us?' She snapped back at me and said, 'No, stupid, it wouldn't be good for us.' I never heard her talk to me like that. It made me feel like trash."

 I could tell his pride was still hurt from what must have been cutting words to his ears. He continued. "She said if she gets divorced, she'll lose half of everything they own. That was the first time she ever spoke to me that way, especially after all I did for her. It made me feel really bad, ya know what I mean? It really hurt my feelings. It sounded as if she __."

Ben interrupted. "Was she a temp?"

"Yes, at first. But from what Veronica told me, she was only one for about six months; then got promoted as his personal secretary. That's what made Veronica suspicious, when he added her to his permanent payroll. All his other secretaries were temps. That way he didn't have to pay them benefits."

"OK. Why was the girl killed?"

"Like I said, Veronica thought she was going to lose a lot of money. I don't know why she was worried. We still would have had plenty. The business was really picking up again."

"How did she do it, or weren't you there when it happened?"

"Yes, I was there, but I didn't know she was going to do it at the time."

"Go on. Describe to me what took place."

"Veronica called her at the office one day and told her Joel wanted her to bring some blank stock forms to the shore. His flight was delayed by the storm coming, and he was going to go directly there."

"Where was he coming from?"

"I don't know. He was returning from an overnight business trip. I guess Karen knew he was out of town, so she did what she thought Joel asked. She never suspected Veronica knew about the engagement."

"Did she intend to kill her then?"

"I didn't know it at the time, but I went to the house later that afternoon, after I boarded up a few homes for customers preparing them for the storm. At that point- I was totally unaware of Karen coming down, until she knocked at the door."

"What were you doing?"

"I was getting ready to mix a drink at the bar."

"Then what happened?"

"I looked at Karen when she came in and asked, 'Are you prepared to stay until the storm passes. It's supposed to be a bad one?' She said no and handed Veronica the stock forms Joel wanted. She said she didn't have much time and wanted to leave before the storm actually hit.

Veronica insisted she should stay and have a drink. She wanted to talk to her about Joel. She had her hand on the door knob ready to leave, but when Veronica mentioned wanting to talk to her about Joel, she came back and sat down on the sofa. I asked Veronica if she wanted me to make the drinks since I was already standing at the bar. She quickly came over to me, taking my glass that only had ice cubes in it, and told me to sit down with Karen while she mixed them."

"What happened then?"

"I remember Veronica asking her if she wanted soda or water with her highball. When she said soda, I saw Veronica take a small blue bottle from a drawer under the bar and put a few drops in Karen's glass. I thought it may have been some kind of flavoring for a drink. I know Veronica experiments from time to time with them."

When he mentioned her putting a few drops in Karen's glass, Ben and I looked at each other. That must have been when she put the chloral hydrate in the drink, the substance that would render her powerless.

"What did you do after you saw her put the drops in her glass?"

"I took my drink and stepped out on the deck to look at the ocean. If they were going to have a heart- to- heart talk, I didn't want to listen to their conversation."

"Did you hear any of it?"

"When I came in off the deck, they seemed to be having a friendly chat, nothing out of the ordinary. It was as if there was nothing wrong."

"Did Karen say anything to Veronica?"

"No. Like I said, they seemed very friendly to each other."

"Did you see Karen with her drink?"

"Yes, she was sitting on the sofa and took a few sips, and within a few minutes, she started getting drowsy."

"Did she go unconscious?"

"No, she just became drowsy and couldn't even hold the glass, then dropped it on the rug. Karen realized there was something wrong and tried getting to her feet. That's when I realized whatever Veronica put in her drink was causing it. Karen tried again to stand up, but Veronica pushed her back down on the couch."

"There were strangle marks on her neck when she was found, did you make them?"

"No, after Karen got so drowsy where she could hardly defend herself, Veronica turned 180 degrees, and flew into a rage. She started strangling Karen and kept yelling at her, 'You bitch! You bitch! You won't get any of my money.' Karen had her hands around Veronica's neck, trying in vain to break away but couldn't. In fact, after she looked like she was unconscious- Veronica went to the closet and got a scarf. She tied it around her neck and kept tightening it till she stopped breathing."

"So the murder was about money? Was Karen dead at that point?"

"I bent down to feel for a pulse, but there was none. I told Veronica, she's dead. She said, 'Good for the bitch,' then spit on her."

"What happened after that?"

"Veronica untied the scarf and put it back in the closet, just like nothing ever happened."

"What happened next?"

"Veronica yelled at me. 'Carl, don't stand there like a dummy. Close the god damn sliding door.' Then she knelt down and began taking off Karen's clothes, ripping at them like she was disgusted with her. Her face was still red with anger. I remember her saying, 'Look at this, the little whore has her initials on her underwear. I wonder if she did that for Joel.' She was having a hard time getting the panties off and looked up at me again. 'What the hell are you waiting for asshole?' I asked her what she meant.

I think I was still in a state of shock, seeing the change in her. She yelled at me, 'You see me trying to take off her god damn clothes. Help me.' I asked, 'Why are we doing that?' she said, "This gives me an idea."

"What kind of idea?" Carl paused, looking down at the floor with a sigh, remembering the scene that was still fresh in his mind as though it happened yesterday, then continued.

"She said she was going to hide the underwear in the trunk of Joel's car, and then pretend to find them by accident. She told me she would fake an argument loud enough to bring the cops. She said since this little bitch his fiancé- has her initials on her underwear, I don't think he'll make too much of a fuss."

"What happened next?"

"We wrapped the body in a blanket and waited until it got dark. Then I carried Karen's body about a hundred yards down the beach and buried her."

"Were you alone?"

"No, Veronica was with me. In fact, she carried the shovel."

"What did you do after you buried her?"

"We returned to the house and I helped Veronica tidy everything up. I remember talking about planting the clothing in Joel's trunk, but I don't remember everything we talked about. I do remember Veronica saying, 'I just earned us about three quarters of a million bucks tonight.' After we tidied up, she poured us a couple of drinks and acted like nothing ever happened. I remember her attitude. She seemed to be happy she was rid of her."

"What was the girl's name who was blackmailing you, and how did she get into the picture?"

"Her name is Heather- Heather O'Brien."

"Where did she live? Is she from the island?"

"No, she lived just outside of Philadelphia- Bensalem I think. She was renting a small cottage down the beach for two weeks at the end of the summer."

"What happened then?"

"The night we buried Karen we thought we were alone on the beach. We thought with the storm coming there wouldn't be anyone out, but Heather was walking the beach and saw us. She hid behind the sand dunes and watched everything we did. After we buried Karen, we went back to the house as if nothing happened. I stayed with Veronica that night and left in the early hours of the morning before it was daylight."

"When did you learn about Heather O'Brien watching, as you got rid of the body?"

"Around noon that day, Veronica called and asked if we could have lunch together. She said she had something important to show me."

"Where did you meet?"

"We met for lunch at the Dock Side Restaurant. When I walked in, she was already there and seemed very nervous and upset. I asked what was wrong. She told me about us being followed from the beach where we buried Karen, then took a note from her purse to show me. She said, 'Hear read this. I found it shoved under my front door this morning.'

"What did the note read?"

"It was from Heather. She said she was renting a house close by- and saw what we did. The note read, as I recall, 'Meet me at the Oxford Valley Mall outside Philadelphia. It's about the buried treasure at the shore.' There was a phone number Veronica was supposed to call that afternoon.

When she called, Heather said she was walking the beach and saw what we did and described everything to a T- she didn't miss a thing."

"Was there any mention of how much she wanted to keep quiet?"

"Yes, according to Veronica- she wanted $10,000 to keep her mouth shut and $1,500 a month to keep it sealed. I told Veronica to first try offering her less. She might just agree, thinking something is better than nothing, and back off on her original demand. She didn't agree, and said we should pay the entire amount, so I gave her half, $5,000."

"So you've been paying that since September? That's several months ago. Has Veronica's been paying that all along?"

"No, I've been giving her a thousand a month. She put up the rest."

"How were the payments made?"

"The payments were in cash. The first payment- $10,000 was made at the Oxford Valley Mall in Bucks County. I think the second payment of $1,500 was made here on the island. I don't know where the other ones were made."

"I remember Veronica telling me she mentioned to Heather she wasn't familiar with the Oxford Valley Mall, and would rather have the meetings someplace she was more familiar with. Veronica told me she took Heather shopping the first day, and bought her a blouse- like it wasn't even a ransom- just a friendly meeting."

"What do you mean, friendly meeting? Most people who would have to pay blackmail money wouldn't just have a friendly meeting."

"I know, but Veronica never showed her any disrespect. In fact, she met her on another occasion at Lord's and Logan's and bought her something else. I don't recall what it was though."

"Carl, is what you're telling me, without putting words in your mouth, that Veronica may have been planning killing Heather all along-building confidence in their relationship?"

"From what happened tonight, I think so."

"When was the last payment made?"

"Tonight: Veronica called me last week and said she just had a phone call from Heather. She wanted to increase the payment to $2,000 a month. Veronica asked her why the increase? We agreed on $1,500? She told me Heather mentioned she was going to have a dependant, whatever that meant."

"Do you mean she was pregnant?"

"No, I think she was talking about a future husband. Veronica mentioned something about her being engaged."

"Did Veronica agree?"

"Yes, after she told me, she said we'd have to do something about her, or she'll always be a threat."

"Is that when she planned to murder her?"

"I think so. I was there when she made the call."

"When was that, tonight?"

"No: the day before yesterday. She called Heather and told her she would have to come to the shore for her payment. She wasn't feeling well. She had a bad cold."

"Tell me what happened when Heather arrived tonight."

"Veronica asked her to come in."

"Did Veronica offer a drink?

"Yes, she handed her the $2,000 and told her they should have a drink to celebrate Heather's engagement."

"Did you witness her putting anything in Heather's glass?"

"No, Veronica didn't want me to be seen and told me to hide in the closet behind the louver door, so I couldn't see the bar where she mixed the drinks."

"What happened then?"

"Veronica gave her the drink then they sat down on the sofa. When they sat down, I was able to open the closet door slightly without Heather noticing. Her back was toward me."

"Then what happened?"

"Veronica asked about her engagement and who the lucky guy was. Heather seemed to enjoy talking about her boyfriend. She didn't seem very bright. The first sip didn't seem to affect her. She continued talking about her wedding plans. After a few more sips, she began to get drowsy. I think she realized something was wrong with the drink and got to her feet. She was swaying; trying to maintain her balance, then dropped her glass and headed toward the door."

"Did she make it that far?"

"Almost, that's when the fight started."

"You mean Veronica in some way was trying to keep her there?"

"Yes, she grabbed her by the arm and tried to push her back down on the sofa. She had her hands around Heather's throat trying to strangle her."

"Did she succeed?"

"No, Heather was a much bigger and stronger girl. She began to get the best of Veronica, choking her- trying to push her away."

Listening to Carl, I finally realized the reason Veronica had marks around her neck. It was probably from her victim's defending themselves.

Joel- thinking it was from some sort of violent relationship- had it wrong. That's why she blew him off when he questioned her about them. I've heard enough that I wondered how I could have been so wrong.

"So Heather wasn't totally unconscious?"

"No, I guess she hadn't had enough of her drink. Either that or Veronica didn't put in as much as she should have. She was only groggy."

"How did Veronica react, having to fight Heather?"

"When Heather completely broke Veronica's hold from around her neck, she began to strangle Veronica."

"What happened then?"

"Veronica called me to help."

"What did you do?"

"Seeing what was happening, I was already coming out of the closet. I picked up the lamp and hit Heather on the side of the head."

"Was she unconscious then?"

"No, it just knocked her down. As I said, she was a strong girl. I reached down and grabbed her by the neck and picked her up off the floor, then strangled her until she stopped fighting."

"Was she dead at that point?"

With his eyes downcast at the floor troubled by what he did, replied... "I think so. She didn't move."

"What was Veronica doing?"

"After I let her drop back to the floor, Veronica was coughing, still trying to recover from the grip Heather had around her neck. When she recovered, she pounced on Heather's chest, and began strangling her again. She was yelling, 'Bitch! Bitch! Bitch!' __She was even fighting me. After I pulled her off, I had to get her a drink of water. Like a crazy person who wasn't satisfied with the punishment she had, she pounced on her again, punching her face."

"What happened then?"

"She told me to help her to get Heather undressed."

"Why did she do that?"

"She told me about the interview she had with you, when she told you about the underwear she found in Joel's car. She planned to hide these in there too. After that, she told me to take the body and put it where it could easily be found within the next several days."

"For what reason did you want this body where it could be easily discovered?"

"She was going to call the police and tell them there must have been a disturbance in her living room. The lamp was broken, and the large dirt mark on the floor from the tropical plant that was knocked over."

"What purpose would that have served?"

"Knowing you already suspected Joel was abusive, you may have investigated the scene in the living room. She would have led you to look in the direction of suspecting Joel of the murders."

"How would she have done that?"

"She saved a glass that Joel used recently with his fingerprints on it. She said he was such a slob and he never picked up after himself. She was going to put it on the bar with the one Heather used. Veronica was going to point them out to you as you looked over the scene of the disturbance. With Heather's fingerprints on one glass and Joel's on the other, it would have shown that he obviously had her there. Finding the underwear in the trunk of his car and the initials J.S. on the inside of the ring of the dead girl found on the beach, the circumstantial evidence piling up against him would be overwhelming. Joel would have been the prime suspect in both murders. Veronica was hoping for a life sentence."

I listened intently at Carl's confession in disbelief. I realized how cunning, cold and calculating she really was, and how not only Carl, but I was easily drawn in by her- and I wondered how many men in her past she drew into her webs of deceptions.

"Carl: Where did you dump the body?"

"It's partially buried on a vacant lot close by, Bay Avenue and Chestnut Street. I put her in a shallow grave so she could be easily found. That lot's scheduled to be cleared for construction day after tomorrow."

Ben turned off the tape recorder, picked up the phone and called the state police and the medical examiner's office. Looking at Carl, he knew the road ahead for him was going to end only one way- life in prison.

Chapter 8

The door opened from the inner office where Veronica was being held.

"Ben, are you finished with the interview?"

"Yea Kevin, Carl's showing me where the body is. I already called the state police and the M.E. They'll meet me at the scene. I'm taking the camera with me too."

"Do you want me to get a statement from Veronica?"

"I don't think that will be necessary. Carl gave me a pretty good account of the whole thing. She'll be charged with three murders and an accessory to murder. Carl will be charged with one count of homicide and three counts of being an accessory."

Through the partially open door, I could see Veronica tugging at the handcuff around her wrist- the other end fastened to the chair. Hearing what Ben said, she screamed.

"I want a lawyer! Let me call my damn lawyer!"

"Carl, put on your coat and show me where the body is."

After putting on their jackets, they headed out the door. Through the window I could see the headlights of another car pull into the parking lot- It was a state police car with two troopers in it. One went with Ben and the other came inside. It was Jesse Strange, the same trooper who was on the beach, when I found Karen White's body. When he entered the room, he recognized me immediately.

"Your names Ron, right. How are you?"

"Not bad considering this kind of excitement. I witnessed the murder that happened tonight."

"I just spoke to Ben on the parking lot. He told me."

I remarked, "I thought you'd be going with him."

"No my partner is. The M.E. is going to meet them there. They'll check out the scene. Ben told me he wouldn't be very long."

Kevin came out of the adjacent room and put on a fresh pot of coffee. In about an hour, Ben returned with Carl. The state trooper that was with Ben, remained with the coroner.

Kevin asked, "Is the body where he buried her?"

"Yes, it's only partially covered. From what I could see, there's dried blood on the side of her head and marks from when she was strangled around her neck. The visible evidence coincides with the account Carl gave. "

"Has Carl been formally charged?"

"Not yet, I wanted to see the body first. As soon as I get my jacket off, I'll start the paperwork."

"Has the medical examiner been notified?"

"Yes, he was there shortly after I got there. They already took the body."

"Carl, step over here, I have to get a set of your fingerprints."

As Ben inked and rolled each finger over an identification card, Carl's eyes welled up with tears. I could tell it was bothering Ben too, having to do something that was gnawing at his inner soul... rolling his friends fingerprints on a card. A card that would forever change Carl's existence and more than likely, a one way ticket to a life sentence, that would confine his building talents, to an eight by ten cell. A ruined family- an ex-wife with two children cast aside for the likes of someone as treacherous as Veronica- And for what? __Money!

I thought if she had married Carl as he was hoping, he might have been a victim of another plot, just as she planned for her husband. She was capable of luring me in easy enough. Her whole existence is about her own comfort and money. I realized how ridiculous I must have sounded offering her my humble abode for refuge from what I believed was an abusive husband. She must have laughed inwardly, knowing that I was hooked and completely vulnerable.

She counted on my affection of fearing for her safety that led me to believe Joel was a serial killer. She was right. I fell right into her scheme. Then I remembered about Joel. With everything that happened, I wondered if I should call him. When we parted at his apartment in the city, he gave me his phone number.

"Ben… Do you think I should call Joel?"

"I wouldn't, not right now. I have to get her processed. I don't think she's going to give me a statement, so it won't take long. A matron from the prison at Barnegat City has to be notified to come here to transport her. On second thought, I think I should call Joel myself. Do you happen to have his number?"

"Yes, here's his card. He gave it to me when we met."

"Thanks, I don't want to say too much on the phone. They're some things I want to discuss with him first."

After Ben was through with Carl, he put the handcuffs on him.

"Kevin, take Carl over to Barnegat Detention Facility. I'll phone and let them know you're coming. Here's the preliminary paperwork. Tell them I'll bring the full charges sheet as soon as I'm finished."

"Can they admit him without all the paperwork?"

"With the charge sheet you have, that will be enough to hold him for 24 hours. That will be plenty of time for the district attorney to charge him formally."

Ben looked at the advancing clock. "I'll have the rest of the paperwork finished in a few hours. I'll run it over to them myself when I'm finished. Do you feel comfortable taking Carl yourself?"

Kevin looked at Carl. "Yes, I don't think he'll be any trouble."

Carl raised his downcast eyes. "Ben… I won't be any trouble."

Kevin escorted Carl to the door, and just before he stepped out, he turned and said, "Ben, I'm sorry I had to put you through all this. I really am."

"Carl, I feel bad for you- and your family. What really bothers me- we'll never again be friends, only acquaintances. That's the real shame."

With a dejected look, Ben walked to the office door and watched as Kevin escorted Carl down the darkened hall and out the front door of the building.

I went to the window and watched as they crossed the parking lot to an awaiting patrol car. After placing Carl in the back seat, they drove away.

"Ron, I have to bring Veronica in here to get a statement. She probably won't say anything, but to avoid a confrontation, could you step into the other office when I bring her in?"

"No problem. I'm probably the last person she wants to see. Let me know when I can come out."

When Ben opened the door, Veronica stared at me with contempt. Passing in the doorway she mumbled something under her breath, but I couldn't distinguish what she said. I knew for certain it wasn't something complimentary, so I dismissed it. Before I closed the door, I heard Ben say,

"Mrs. Simmons, you don't have to give me a statement unless you want to. Step over here. I have to take your photograph. Front and profile, then I have to take your fingerprints."

Knowing her now the way I do, I imagined as he took her picture, she realized a weight- a real anchor had just been attached to her. A cold, plain black and white photo, front and profile; sharing the same small piece of developing paper that will be her passport. Without expression and quite unappealing, she stood still while Ben took an ink pad and card from a drawer. Standing in silence, she looked down at her fingers, as he rolled them one at a time over the ink pad, then transferring them to a card with her arrest number. It was an official seal, and conformation, that her shopping days at Lord's and Logan's were over. No more luncheons with friends. No more standing out on her deck looking out at the ocean. For all intents and purposes, she might just as well be dead, dead as Heather and as dead as Karen White. Their lives were over, where Veronica will have to spend the rest of her life wondering whether it was all worth it. With Carl's testimony, she would never see the light of day, and if by chance she did, she would be so old no one would even notice her. It must have finally registered with her that this was real. She suddenly blurted out, "All I'll say is I want a lawyer!"

"I'll let you call after I'm finished."

I couldn't hear any distinguishable conversation coming from the room, but she couldn't contain her rage any longer. Then burst out again in frustration. "Why are you only taking Carl's statement? He's the one that murdered those girls. He's a sex degenerate. He gets a real thrill out of doing it. You only believe him because he's your friend. You have no proof. How would I have the strength to strangle anyone_. Ron already told you he saw Carl strangle that girl tonight."

Ben interrupted in a lower voice. "Look, I think you'll be better off not saying anything."

"Okay: You damn hicks from these small communities always stick together. I want to call my lawyer."

Knowing Ben was already frustrated having to fingerprint and photograph a close friend. I could imagine he was fighting back the anger from her words- words that were cutting deep. About 10 minutes later, I heard a female voice- someone had just entered the office.

"Hello, Officer Davis, I'm Carol Wilson. I'm a matron from the prison. Is this the woman I have to transport?"

"Yes it is. Wait just a minute. I'll give you the paperwork."

"What's the charge?"

"For right now, it's being an accessory to a murder. I already finger-printed her. Here's a copy."

I could hear Ben say goodbye and the outer door close. Stepping from the room, I told Ben, "I was listening to her rant about Carl being the murderer. Even after all this, she's still lying."

"Not so fast Ron. The only word we have is Carl's about her drug-ging the victims. I have to get back to the house and see if I can find that bottle of Chloral hydrate. If I can find it, I'm hoping her fingerprints are still on the bottle. I don't have a key to the house. That's why I told you to wait. I'm going to call Mr. Simmons now and get him down here."

"Ben, maybe if I call, it will get him down here quicker. When I spoke to him at his apartment, he still had feelings for her. I know he did. I wouldn't want him to screw up your investigation by going there first, and destroying evidence."

"Maybe you're right. Here's his card."

Taking it, I dialed the number. It was picked up on the second ring, and a voice that sounded half asleep said, "Hello, who is it?"

"Joel, this is Ron. Ron Bennett."

"What can I do for you? Ron. What the hell time is it?"

"It's 2:30. I think you better come to the police station in Beach Haven. Something happened at your shore house tonight."

The words shook him from his half sleep, and he was anxious for an explanation. He asked, "What's wrong? What happened? Is it some-thing about Veronica? Is she hurt?"

I knew he was fully awake at this point. "No, she's not hurt, but I think you should come here."

He paused. "I'll be there in about an hour."

I was surprised he was so upset. It told me he was still interested in her.

"Ben, would you mind if I use one of your typewriters and some paper? I want to jot down some notes for my news story?"

"Sure the blank papers on the shelf in the cabinet over the desk."

I poured a cup of fresh coffee Kevin made before leaving; then sat down at one of the desks. Ben watched as I was hammering out the events of what took place, then remarked. "I should have let you do the typing. I would have been finished an hour and a half ago."

I smiled. "I never thought to ask if you wanted me to. I was so mesmerized by Carl's account, I didn't think about it. Besides, you have it recorded."

After 40 minutes of forming the story for the news article, I saw the headlights of a car coming into the parking lot. Thinking it might be Kevin coming back, I resumed typing. When the door swung open I looked up. To my surprise, it was Joel. He must have driven 90 miles an hour.

It's only been 40 minutes since I called him. He was nervous and pale, anticipating what was going to be said. He didn't have the demeanor or confidence I saw when I met him at the bar or when we went to his apartment.

It struck me. This guy's isn't still mildly concerned for his wife; he's still deeply in love with her. He may have wanted to get a divorce over what was transpiring in his marriage, but there was no doubt in my mind, given the chance, he would have put it all behind and started over again.

Quickly looking around the room without seeing her, remarked, "What happened? Where is she?"

Ben asked, "Are you Joel, Veronica's husband?"

"Yes, where is she?"

"She's been taken to Barnegat Light Correctional Institution, Women's Division."

"Why, what did she do? What's this all about, Ron?"

I began to tell him what had taken place when Ben interrupted. "Joel, she's being charged with conspiracy to commit murder- one, possibly two counts of homicide."

Joel's expression was disbelief at what he was being told.

"Veronica? My Veronica:"

"Yes, I'm afraid so. Carl Dunn the contractor was also booked on the same charges."

"Why, Carl Dunn?"

"They both had a hand in killing a girl tonight in your house at the beach." He looked in my direction, "It was witnessed by Ron here."

"Ron, you saw them do it?"

"Yes, they were shadows behind the drapes at the house. I thought it was you, strangling the girl who was killed. To be quite frank, I thought you were the one responsible for murdering the girls here at the shore."

"Why would you think that?"

"It was Veronica leaving me small hints and innuendos, letting my affection for her take over my reasoning."

Ben interrupted, "Carl gave a statement. He told me the dead girl on the beach four months ago was your fiancé. Was she?"

"Yes, she was."

"Then why didn't you come forward and tell us who the girl was?"

"I was afraid, afraid that Veronica may have had something to do with it."

"Then you suspected she was capable of murder?"

"Yes, especially after I asked her for a divorce. In fact, I asked several times. Every time I asked, it became a battle of very heated words."

"The blue sapphire ring, was that an engagement ring?"

"Yes, I was still married to Veronica, and we didn't want to flaunt our engagement in anyone's face. The detectives were in touch with me several weeks ago. They discovered I purchased it in center city."

"We're you the one responsible for the bruises Ron saw on Veronica's neck?"

"No. I never laid a hand on her. I saw her with bruises on her neck and on her back several times. When I asked about them, she gave me a short answer and dismissed my question, as if I annoyed her or she didn't hear me. At first I thought she might be having an extra marital relationship that was a little dangerous, but she had them before, and I no longer loved her but still cared. I related all this to Ron, in our conversation at my apartment."

Ben looked at me to verify his statement.

"That's true Ben. He did tell me about them."

Listening to Carl's statement, he said Heather and Veronica were locked in a strangle hold of each other. We suddenly realized they may have been marks from victims, trying in vain to protect themselves. Like the marks that were beginning to appear on Veronica's neck tonight. With his obvious concern for Veronica with the phone call, I realized he was also lying about not loving her any longer, but only mildly concerned.

"What do you mean when you said she had affairs before? You didn't love your wife any longer, but didn't tell us the girl you were engaged to was the dead girl on the beach. Why not:"

"At the time, I only mildly suspected Veronica may have known something about it. It must have happened just after the last time Veronica and I had a heated argument, about getting a divorce."

When he said that, Ben and I looked at each other again, realizing Carl was telling the truth.

"Did Carl give an account of how they killed Karen?"

"Yes, he told us Veronica found out about the engagement ring and lured her to the shore house by telling her you wanted some blank stock forms. When she got there, Veronica put something in a drink that made her unconscious; then strangled her. Carl told me they buried her on the beach, and while they were doing it, they were seen by the girl who was killed tonight. She was blackmailing them. Did Veronica ever give you a reason to think she was capable of murder?"

"I don't know whether telling you this would indicate whether or not she was capable of murder, but a little more than a year ago, Veronica began questioning me about always hiring young girls as secretaries. I told her it was flattering you're jealous, but her having extramarital affairs and worrying about me using young secretaries boarders on being hypocritical. I told her she didn't have anything to worry about. I wasn't going anywhere. It hurt me to tell her I was aware of her affairs, but I still loved her and hoped she would change. It must've gotten the best of her trying to stay young."

"What do you mean trying to stay young?"

"Since she turned 30, she was always looking in the mirror counting imperfections on her face and constantly going to skin doctors who cost a fortune for treatments."

Ben looking deep in thought, toying with a pencil on the desk, asked. "Joel, would you mind if I recorded this conversation?"

"No, I wouldn't..."

Ben reached down and turned on the recorder once again, then continued questioning.

"You mentioned the argument about getting the bruises, occurred a little more than a year ago. Did you have any secretaries who suddenly quit or just didn't show up at the job?"

"Yes, I had two secretaries who were from temporary employment agencies. They both worked for about three months, then just stopped showing up for some reason. I phoned their company, but they just sent out another temp, and I never thought to question it."

"Karen White. Was she a temp?"

"She was at first, but then she was so efficient, I hired her full time. I think it was a combination of both her work- and my becoming interested in her."

"Do you have a record of the temps who worked for you the last two years?"

"Yes, that information would be in the office. I'll bring it down in the morning."

I knew what Ben was thinking. He was wondering whether he could make an identification of the other dead girls- something they hadn't been able to do.

"Joel, I have to get back in your house. I can either get you to sign a written statement allowing me, or I can get a warrant."

"No problem. I'll sign a permission form. What are you looking for?"

"There's a small bottle I'm interested in. Carl said he saw Veronica take it out of a drawer at the bar. That: and possibly a few glasses with finger prints on them."

Putting on his jacket, Ben turned and said, "Ron, do you want to come with us?"

"Thanks, Ben, I'd like to."

When we reached the house, Joel unlocked the door and we went in. Ben went straight to the bar and opened the drawer. After he looked in, he put on a pair of rubber gloves and retrieved a small blue bottle. Holding it up to the light, he examined its contents. Taking a few small plastic bags from his pocket, he put the bottle in one, then, gathered two glasses that were on the bar, and one from the coffee table. Putting them in separate bags, he marked them as evidence and noted their placement at the crime scene.

I looked behind the bar where I discovered a wine bottle, and mentioned it to Ben. Gently picking it up, he placed it in another evidence bag. I happened to glance over to the far end of the bar and saw a small dish washer for bar glasses.

"Ben, did you check the dishwasher?" I Pointed to it.

"No, I didn't think of it. Thanks."

Opening the door, he found a few ash trays and several glasses. Carefully picking them up one at a time, he held them up to the light examining them for fingerprints, and put them in separate plastic bags.

"They haven't been washed. Joel, would you mind if I came back later and took some more pictures? I'm anxious to get back to the station and get some of the paperwork started."

I looked at Joel who didn't answer Ben's question. He seemed to be absorbed in his own world, saddened by what happened. Slowly looking around the room, he seemed to be reminiscing about a time when he and Veronica had a few good times together. Possibly, remembering an enjoyable romantic evening in front of the fire place. Laughing and sipping a glass of wine. All of a sudden, I felt a little guilty seeing the relationship from the other side. He was a guy that gave his all and got very little in return. My conscience got the best of me.

Ben repeated his words a little more authoritative. "Joel, do you mind if I come back at daylight to take more pictures of Veronica's car and the inside of the house?"

It seemed to snap him back from thumbing through his album of memories.

"I'm sorry. I didn't hear you. Of course, anything you have to do, you have my permission. In fact, let me get you a key, you can come and go as you please."

"Thanks, I appreciate it. I'm finished here for now. Let's get back to the station."

Joel took a final look around the room, turned off the light and closed the door. Returning to the police station, Ben asked, "Would you want to read Carl's confession?"

"Yes, I would."

As he was reading through the pages, he stopped, shook his head then looked up. "I can't believe this relationship has been going on behind my back for so long." then continued reading.

Ben interrupted, Joel, if there's anything you read in his confession that you think might not be true, tell me, and I can have a separate statement from you. Something the district attorney may need."

Looking up from the confession, Joel said, "Ben, There's a few things I see already." He was laughing lightly, as if to say, what he was reading was an exaggeration.

"It's about building my house and how we became a partnership. Carl has a saintly view of himself. It borders on being an innocent victim of a financial crisis he had no control over."

Ben looked over at him. "What do you mean- the financial meltdown that affected his business?"

"Yes, that's exactly what I mean. Let me finish reading this, and I'll tell you how it really started."

After finishing, he laid the report down on the desk. Consciously, he spoke, but his words seemed to be coming from a subconscious thought.

Shaking his head, laughing, he said, "I can't believe Carl could be such a liar. There's not one word mentioned about him running to the casinos in Atlantic City several times a week, blowing a bunch of money. Money he didn't really have. His ex-wife Carla should be reading this. She'd have a few choice words to say."

I was thinking to myself__. That's right. I read that in the private detectives report. He was following Veronica to the casinos- then lost her in the crowd. She must have been meeting Carl there too.

Ben asked, "So you're telling me Carl's a gambler?"

"That's right- and a poor one at that. That's what caused his financial crisis more than any other outside influences. His ex-wife Carla threatened to leave him several times about it. She wasn't just angry to the point it wasn't private conversation, but outright hostile confrontations about his losses, and it didn't make any difference who was in the room.

I remember on one occasion just before she left him, they were at a party at my house with several of my business associates. The conversation somehow got on the subject of the casinos. She had a few drinks, but seeing her drink on other occasions, it was nothing Carla couldn't handle.

She began a triad of humiliation at Carl that left me and my other guests speechless. In fact, one of my guests was a potential prospect for Carl to be his contractor. He had just purchased a beach front property and wanted Carl to tear it down and erect his new home. After that scene, it was small wonder why he backed away. Shortly after that, Carla took the two kids and left him. It's a shame for Carla. She really put up with a lot."

Ben asked, "Joel, would you mind giving me an official interview? I only asked you if you would allow the recording. I'd like to get this down on paper."

"No problem. I'll sign any paper that gives you permission."

He thanked Joel and took a standard permission paper from his drawer.

"Sign right here!"

After he signed it, Ben continued his interview.

"When Veronica left, she was shouting that Carl was to blame for most of this. I want to make sure I have everyone's statements for the record. For whatever it's worth, it may help with their verdicts."

"No problem, Ben. I just want you to know there's more to this."

Ben turned on the tape recorder again. "Joel, do you mind if I record our conversation?"

"I don't mind." It was recorded. His permission was being sealed on the small reel that was slowly turning, taking in the conversation.

"Start with telling me about your earliest contact with Carl."

"When Veronica and I purchased the house that originally stood where our house is now, we set out to find a contractor. Carl Dunn was the premier builder here in Beach Haven, and he came with high recommendations from the realtor who handled our purchase. We had several meetings with him to discuss the plans of the house and make any last-minute changes in the architecture. He seemed to know what he was talking about and took us around to see some of his earlier accomplishments. After we agreed on him becoming the contractor, it was already late spring. He told us he couldn't begin until late spring the following year. He had that many prior commitments."

"Was there any contact between those incidental meetings other than the construction?"

"Yes, we made it a social event twice. Once we met Carl and his wife for dinner at the Roseberry Inn, here on the island, and once when they invited us down for a spaghetti dinner. I might add, Carla is a great Italian cook."

"Yes, I know, we were great friends. I'm sorry. Go on. When did he start construction of your house?"

"Well, like I said, the time we met for dinner at the Roseberry, Carl told us we'd have to wait until late spring of the following year to get started. That meant it probably wouldn't be finished until late fall or winter, depending on the weather. As we were leaving, Carla mentioned making us dinner two weekends later, and we agreed.

On the drive home, Veronica complained about it taking so long to begin construction. I thought she was going to ask me to find another contractor, but instead, she asked me to give him a cash incentive to put off someone else and start our project sooner. She wanted to be in by mid-summer the following year."

"When did you offer him the proposition?"

"The day we went to his home for the dinner."

Ben stopped momentarily to adjust the microphone of the recorder. We were both listening intently to his account of events.

"Tell me about it."

"When we were in his living room, I asked, Carl, what would it take to put one of your other projects on hold and start ours late this year? Veronica wants to be in by mid-summer next year."

He was surprised at my question and looked at me. I could tell he didn't quite know what to say. I remember he just stared at me for a few moments, then replied_, 'I'm not sure what you're asking me to do, Joel.' I knew he understood the question. He just didn't know the figure of money that was involved in my request. I told him to consider it a bribe. How much would it take to put someone else on hold and start our project? ...I told him I was willing to give him $20,000 cash for the favor. I took the money from my inside pocket and laid it on the coffee table- $20,000 new crisp one thousand dollar bills. I remember him sitting back in his seat, looking at me, then down at the cash, taking it off the table.

He said, 'I think I can begin in October. I can guarantee you'll be in by mid-summer next year_ according to the weather, maybe even sooner."

"That settled the deal for the present, but I didn't know at the time he was gambling as much as he was. I have to say, though, he did what he promised and began in mid- October."

"When did you become partners?"

With a surprised look at Ben, realizing he knew about that, remarked, "Sometime in early spring. I think it was April. One day Veronica and I made a surprise visit to the shore house.

At that point it was what contractor's call, 'under roof.' Everything on the outside was done at that point, and the construction since February was all dedicated to the interior. When we got to the job site, several men from his construction company, were sitting around inside. When we walked in, they stood up, surprised to see us.

"I asked the foreman, 'Where's Carl? The last time we were here the electrician was supposed to have started. What's the hold up?'

"He told me the electrician was held up on another job site and couldn't get there. I asked him again where Carl was. He told me he should be there any minute, and wanted to know if he was expecting me. I told him no and that I just taken a chance and drove down."

Just then Carl walked in and I asked him, 'Carl, why hasn't the electrician been here? He was supposed to have started three weeks ago?' He told me the electrician wanted more money than he originally asked for, so he was waiting him out.

"What do you mean waiting him out?" Ben asked.

"To quote Carl: 'He wants $5,000 more than he originally asked or he was going to wait out his time on the contract, just long enough to make his deadline."

"What do you mean make his deadline?"

"When construction jobs of this magnitude are written, they're subject to time deadlines. That's an approximate of when their part of the job begins and how much time it takes to complete. That way, it doesn't hold up the other trades with their work_ insulators, sheet rockers, finish carpenters and painters. I asked Carl, 'Why didn't you just pay him?' His reply was surprising."

"What do you mean surprising?"

He said, 'I told him to go fuck himself. I'll wait you out.'

"Couldn't he just hire another electrician?" Ben asked.

"That's what I told him, but he said he already gave him $5,000 as a down payment and didn't want him taking unfair advantage of me."

"What did you do then?"

"I peeled out $5,000 from my pocket and handed it to him. I told him, 'Go get the fuckin' guy and get my work done.' He saw I was pissed off and didn't hesitate to answer."

He told me he knew which job he's working on and went right over to give it to him. I told him I'd be back next week to check. I also told him that's why I'm paying him. I don't want to have to get involved. I'm too busy. That's when Veronica spoke up in what sounded like his defense.

"What do you mean by his defense?"

"It sounded like she was sympathetic to Carl's problem. I remembered her saying, 'I think Carl's doing his best. It's not his fault if the electrician didn't get here. If you don't have time to run down, I can make the trip and let you know if there's any further holdup.' "I was satisfied with that for the present and let it go at that."

"Do you think that was when they got together, her coming down looking over the project?" Ben asked.

"I don't think so- not at that time. I remember asking him once if he was secretly seeing Veronica. He told me no, and for some reason I believed him."

"Did he solicit any more money to get the house finished?"

"The work wasn't going as fast as I thought and one day I asked him, what was wrong?"

"Did he ask you for more money?"

"Not actually. That's when he told me he was stretched with money, trying to get the jobs finished he already started, including mine. That's when Veronica stepped in. She asked me to bargain for more amenities to our house that was nearing completion and convinced me to ask for a percentage of his business for a cash bail- out. He was in debt up to his ears, and I knew it. He couldn't borrow any more, and suppliers were closing their doors to him. He was, for all intents and purposes, bankrupt. I threw him a life line."

"What did he say to your offer?"

"How could he refuse? He was between a rock and a hard place. I gave him a $100,000 just to keep his head above water. I did let him know, in no uncertain terms, that I would be closely monitoring my investment. He laughed when I said it, but I knew he realized I was serious."

"With all your other business, how were you able to monitor things?"

"Actually, if Carl and Veronica weren't secretly seeing each other up till then, I guess you could say it was me who pushed them together. I trusted her, so I let her handle the partnership."

"I know from Ron you were having her followed by a detective." Taking a paper from his desk drawer, he read it. "A Detective Brown, Private Investigator. When did that begin?"

He looked surprised when Ben asked him that question, casting a glance in my direction. He knew he could have only gotten that information from one person-me.

Joel continued. "A little more than a year and a half ago, she was getting out of the shower when I noticed a few bruises on her arms and around her neck. I asked her about them, and she acted as though she didn't hear me. Our marriage was already on a slippery slope at that time, and I thought she may have been involved in a relationship that was a little violent. That's when I hired the detective and had her followed."

Joel looked in my direction. "That's how I knew Ron here was involved with her. I also knew he was here with Veronica at the police station. The private detective took pictures of them leaving."

"Joel, I never told Ben that. I only mentioned the private investigator. The rest he's learning from you."

"Well, at any rate, having her followed didn't give me a clue to who was abusing her. At the time she was seen with three other men."

"Do you know who they were?"

"One was a client that Ron did a corruption story on. He's in Federal Prison in Upstate Pennsylvania. The other two from the detective's report were short lived relationships. His report was pretty complete. I can say he failed in one respect, though."

Ben asked, "What was that?"

"He never suspected Carl, and neither did I."

"Did you have an argument over underwear she found in the trunk of your car?"

"Yes, that was in the driveway of our home outside Philadelphia. We had a hell of a battle over it. She made a scene so loud the neighbor had to call the police. I'm sure you can check that out. They should've made a report, but I swear to you, I don't know how they got there."

After Joel said it, Ben and I looked at each other, remembering Carl's confession about Veronica putting them there, then creating a fuss loud enough to bring the police.

"Joel: did you and Veronica always have marital problems, or were they something that began the last several years?"

"No, in fact we had a great marriage until several years ago, around the time my father passed away. He had quite a few high- roller clients in stocks from years ago- really trusted. When dad died, I had to build their confidence handling their portfolios. People who are wealthy are extremely cautious, and it took a lot of doing- financial moves that would convince them their confidence in me wouldn't be misplaced. I had to put in long hours and had many meetings just to satisfy them. In my business, it's easy to lose clients. It's built on trust of someone else handling your money. At the time I wasn't home a lot."

"Is that when you first noticed the change?"

"No, it seemed to begin when she hit her early 30's. I would see her every morning constantly looking in the mirror, counting the wrinkles on her face. She began using all kinds of facial creams. I used to send her flowers for no special occasion, just to let her know my real affection still existed. I used to tell her that's part of the aging process. We'll grow old together gracefully. Every time I said it, she would look at me as if to say, 'I'll prove you wrong.'

That's when she started making appointments with face doctors who cost a fortune. The first one she went to I believe she had an affair with, but that's only an opinion. His bill sure didn't reflect any hint of familiarity. He was expensive."

"Why was she going there? Did he do plastic surgery?"

"No, like I said, she tried to hide the wrinkles. She would go about every month and get any kind of new skin treatment to fight the aging process. I remember being in a drug store with her once, when she asked a woman behind the counter for a certain kind of facial product. The woman behind the counter wasn't familiar with that product and looked confused after Veronica tried to explain what it was- Something that would prevent wrinkles. "

"A few older Italian men taking shelter from the rain- were standing close enough to hear Veronica's conversation. They looked like a group of mustache Pete's- right off the boat- oversized Jeff hats and all. With wisdom that only comes from longevity in life and the lack of tact getting one's point across, one of the men said in perfect broken English: 'Hey lady, if you wanna' die without wrinkles, you gotta' die before you're 25.' It brought a laugh from the group and two other people waiting for their prescriptions to be filled. Indignant over the remark, she gave him a dirty look- then hurriedly walked out the door. As hard as I tried, I couldn't contain my laughter, and the ride the rest of the way home was less than serene."

"Is that when she switched to more expensive treatments?"

"Yes, when she turned 32, I think it really started to bother her. She was really getting paranoid. I think she realized she was fighting a losing battle. That's when she really began accusing me of always hiring temp secretaries who were young and attractive. It really got bad the last several years. I remember shaving one day standing at the vanity in our bathroom. She came in the door and went to her sink, then began examining her face in the mirror. Suddenly, for no reason, she turned and looked at me, then started screaming. 'I know you're seeing those sluts you're hiring. Why don't you admit it?'

Joel continued... "At the time, I knew she was having the other relationships, and I gave her a sarcastic look. I told her, 'Look Veronica, you
being jealous of me hiring young secretaries is flattering, but somewhat
hypocritical.

I don't have a choice as to who the agency sends. As long as they
do the job, I really don't care. You don't have to worry, I'm not going
anywhere.' I think when I said 'hypocritical,' she realized I knew about her
sordid relationships and let it go at that."

Ben asked, "I'm going to ask you a hypothetical question. Do you
think that's what started her killing the girls? If it comes down to that,
being jealous and removing what she thought was competition? That's
the only motive I can see?"

"Unofficially of course, that may have been the reason. There
wouldn't be any other. She never really knew any of them. She only saw
them once in awhile."

"Do you have anything else you could relate about Carl's involve-
ment with Veronica?"

"Not really. Like I said, I never suspected they had that close a relationship. There is one incident that I forgot to mention though."

"What's that?"

Pausing for a moment as if he was trying to recall, Joel said, "Now
that I'm thinking about it, I always thought it was Carl's gambling that
caused the problems with his wife. Maybe it wasn't."

"What do you mean?"

"Like I explained before, we were pretty close. We spent a lot of
time together. Veronica and Carla were becoming very good friends.
Veronica took her on shopping sprees several times, sometime making
it an all- day affair, having lunch in one of the fancier restaurants. All of a
sudden, it stopped. I didn't know why at the time- whether it was something said or Carla suspecting at that point Veronica had an unusual
interest in Carl. I don't know."

Thinking for a moment, "I asked Veronica once- 'Why the sudden change? Are you and Carla having problems?' It seemed like Carla

always found an excuse not to be able to attend anything. Sometimes, Carl would come by himself and make an excuse for his wife not being there."

"If there's nothing else to add, I'll turn off the recorder." Ben said.

"Unless you have a specific question on our relationship, I have nothing to add."

Reaching over to turn off the recorder... "No, I don't have any more questions."

Joel replied, "Well, I have a few. What's going to happen to Veronica now?"

"As she was being taken out- she was yelling that Carl was the one who was guilty and asking how she have the strength to strangle any of those girls. It's shaping up to be a battle between the two of them, as to which one's guilty. We do know from the forensic report, the body of the girl found on the lot at the bait and tackle shop, Karen, and I suspect the impending coroner's report from Heather, the girl killed tonight, had an overdose of chloral hydrate in them.

"I believe that's what's in the small blue bottle I took from the drawer behind the bar. Chemical analyses will reveal what's in it. At any rate, they'll take pictures of any bruises Veronica might have at the detention center. That's standard procedure. I didn't look, but if there are any, that might be in line with what Carl said about the struggle. They were choking each other. They'll both be charged with the homicide that happened tonight, along with being an accessory to premeditated murder. They'll also be charged with various other offenses the district attorney might add. If they're found guilty, they'll be away for a long time, and that's for sure. Do you want to visit Veronica? I can call the Matron at the facility and arrange it?"

"Thanks, not right now, I think I'll wait till tomorrow."

The night went by so quickly. When I looked out the window, dawn was breaking.

Listening to Ben's interview, my conscious was bothering me more now than ever, and looking at Joel had a profound effect on me. It wasn't the fact that he just discovered his wife was a murderer and was going to be tried for her crimes. It was something else? Was it inside my own mind that made me feel like I had to say something to cleanse my soul, something that would extinguish this uneasy feeling of being in Joel's company? Looking at his face so forlorn and helpless, I had to speak, I had to say something.

"Look Joel. I'm sorry if I caused you any additional grief. I know I said it before. At first I just thought she was in a failed marriage, and you were abusive and she wanted to leave you, but didn't quite know how. I won't lie. The more I was in her company; the more I became physically attracted by her beauty and charm. I meant you no personal harm. She was very believable."

His eyes were down cast through most of Ben's interview, and only looked up on several occasions. I waited for some sort of reply, something that would lift this burden of guilt off my shoulders. He hesitated to speak and slowly lifted his downcast eyes off the floor and just looked at me, examining the words he was going to use. Suddenly, as if a weight was lifted off my conscience he replied.

"No, Ron, on the contrary. Reading Carl's confession, I know now she was capable of doing anything. I probably would have wound up in jail serving a life sentence for both murders, or at the very least spent most of my life there. Worst case scenario, she might have had me killed. Knowing what I know now, I wouldn't put it past her. She proved she was perfectly capable of doing anything."

I felt a little better. It was like being exonerated, but saw he was still very much in anguish from the event. I didn't know whether he realized I was uncomfortable with my feelings and said it just trying to make me feel better.

Ben asked Joel again, "Do you want to see your wife? I can call the detention center where she's being held and let them know you'll be stopping by?"

"No thanks, Ben, I'd rather wait until morning."

Getting up to leave, I was gathering the notes I had written about what took place. Ben handed me a folder.

"Here, Ron, you have a stack of notes there. This will keep them from getting lost."

Kevin returned to the office, and Ben introduced him to Joel.

"Kevin, this is Joel Simmons, Mrs. Simmons' husband. How did everything go at the detention center?"

"Your wife raised a lot of hell when she first got there, but after a while, she finally calmed down. Here, Ben." Kevin reached into his inner jacket pocket, pulled out a brown envelope and laid it on Ben's desk.

"What's this?"

"They're photos of marks around Mrs. Simmons' neck. The matron who came here to pick her up took them. She said the district attorney would probably want them put in the envelope along with your report,"

Ben opened the envelope, thumbing through several photos.

Joel asked, "Ben, do you mind if I take a look at them?"

"I don't mind. Here!"

As he was looking through the pictures, Ben asked, "Unofficially, of course, are the marks similar to the ones you saw on her neck before?"

"Unofficially Ben, Yes."

Kevin asked, "Hey Ben, where's the coffee?"

"I've been busy with an interview with Mr. Simmons. I haven't had time to put it on."

"That's alright. I'll do it."

As Kevin was setting up the coffee pot, he turned to Ben.

"It will sure feel good getting the pressure off. The mayor should be really happy."

Joel asked, "Ben, what's going to happen now?"

"Well she'll be charged formally by the district attorney within the next few hours, then arraigned. A court date with a preliminary hearing will be set, which I believe her lawyer, whoever he is, will certainly wave. After that, a court date will be set. You and Ron both will be called to testify. Who's her lawyer?"

"I have a personal lawyer George Goldstein. He's under retainer, but he's a business and tax man. I'm sure his office has people who are criminal lawyers. That's obviously what she's going to need- and a damn good one at that."

"I'm sure it is. She's going to put up a fight about who killed that girl, but either way, that's something they'll battle in court between lawyers. One thing I can guarantee for sure- They'll both be behind bars for a very long time."

Saying that was like a knife to Joel's heart, and his face reflected the stinging words. I thought to myself- even after all that, he still cares.

"Ben, you asked me before whether I wanted to see her. Well, I changed my mind. Could you make the call and let whoever I have to see, know I'd like to stop on the way home."

"No problem Joel." Ben picked up the receiver and dialed the number.

Kevin remarked... "Who wants coffee?"

Joel replied, "I think I'll take a cup before I leave. I'm not looking forward to this trip."

"Ron: how about you?"

"I think I'll have one too. Then I have to hit the road. I have a story I have to write. Joel, I guess the next time I see you will be at the trial."

"I guess so."

Ben took me aside. "Ron, I know you probably have been told this before, being an eye witness to corruption trials, but if I were you, I wouldn't discuss this thing. It's for certain that's one of the questions their defense attorneys will ask- whether you talked about it. Best, not to get in the middle of that, stay with what you actually know. Forget what you heard from the interviews here."

After having coffee- Joel and I walked out together. Getting into our different cars, we left.

Chapter 9

Hurrying back to my apartment, I took Daisy for a walk- then started in on the story. Halfway through, I paused, trying to figure out just how much I should elaborate. The room was quiet, for the exception of me clicking my pen against my chin- a habit I had when writing.

I couldn't reveal who was to blame for the murders. As far as I actually knew, it could have been a combination of both. I knew whatever I exposed here would come up in the trial, and I didn't want to give a wrong impression. All I could do was stick to the facts, and the facts are__ I saw someone being assaulted by shadows on a window, and she wound up dead. I thought to myself, it's like telling half a story, something I hated doing, getting it out piecemeal. But I had no choice.

A week went by, and I finally received a subpoena for the following week. I phoned the district attorney to ask if the jury had already been selected. She told me the selection would be completed by the end of the week. Ben was right. Veronica's lawyer waived the preliminary hearing.

The following week when I entered the court house at Barnegat City, the first person I saw was Joel.

"Hi, Ron, I saw your story in the newspaper. For all the excitement that night, it was kind of vague. It looks like this is going to be a long trial."

"Well, I took Ben's advice. I didn't put anything in the story I didn't actually see."

"I figured that was the case."

"Joel, have you seen Veronica since that morning?"

"I visited her that morning, that's all. She looked pretty distraught. I know she hired a criminal lawyer from my attorney's office. I spoke to him. He said he knew you."

"What's his name?"

"Sam. Sam Denker. Do you remember him?"

"Yes, he's one of the best. I was involved in a few corruption stories with him. That client we talked about before that you had- Howard Krass- well Sam Denker was his defense attorney. He grilled the hell out of me. For what it's worth, I don't know how much good it's going to do Veronica, but we'll see."

The door of the court room swung open, and we entered, taking seats near the front. The district attorney came up to me, extended her hand.

"My name is Carmen Ortega. I'm the assistant district attorney who will be trying this case."

A Spanish woman about 5 foot 2, around 30 years old, slim with pitch- black shoulder length hair, she wore a cream- colored blouse with a dark skirt and matching vest.

"I'm Ron Bennett. This is Joel Simmons, the defendant's husband. Miss Ortega, I remember you from one of my corruption stories. Part of it took place in New Jersey. The trial was held in Camden."

"I thought your face was familiar. I remember that case. Howard Krass was the defendant, correct?"

"That's correct. Howard Krass was one of Joel's clients."

"I hope he still isn't one, Mr. Simmons."

"No, luckily, I dropped him as a client six months before he was arrested for insider trading with another broker."

"Mr. Simmons, will you excuse us. Ron, I'd like to have a word with you out in the hall."

Getting up from my seat following her, I happened to look back at Joel. He seemed to be bothered at her request to go outside for our conversation, and watched as we made our way through the spectators that were coming in. Once we reached the hall outside the courtroom, she abruptly turned and said, "How much have you confided in Mr. Simmons since the defendant was arrested?"

"I haven't seen or spoken to him since that night. Why?"

"While you were entering the courtroom, I overheard you asking if he saw his wife since then."

"That's true. I was asking as a matter of fact. Why?"

"Because he's a liar, that's why! I've been to the Women's Detention Center a few times. His name, as well as her lawyer's name, is written in the visitors log quite a few times. Be careful what you say. I wouldn't want you to commit perjury. That lawyer costs big money. He'll look for any angle to get her a reduced sentence or try to get her acquitted."

"Acquitted? Are you serious?"

"Very serious: They're accusing each other. Your testimony will be the most damaging, and the way it looks now, Carl seems to be the one in the hot seat. His whole confession doesn't count for much, other than his own protection. You're only an eye witness to the shadow of a man strangling a woman, then the brief movement across the drapes of another shadow."

"What about the confession from Carl Dunn?"

"That's only his word against hers- difficult to prove without corroboration. Be direct with your testimony. Don't elaborate."

"Thanks for the warning, Miss Ortega."

After returning to the courtroom, I took my same seat next to Joel. He leaned over and asked, "What was that all about?"

"Oh, nothing much- She just wanted me to read over the statement I gave Ben that night. After I finished, she asked if I had anything else to add."

"Why the meeting in the hallway, you could have read it right here."

"I don't know. Maybe she didn't want me reading it here, with all these people talking. There are a lot of people here. This is a pretty big case. Do you know any of them?"

"Yes." He pointed to the other side of the room. "There are a few of Veronica's friends and two of her not- so- close relatives. I think they're cousins. They're probably here for moral support."

I chuckled. "Why haven't they come over to speak to you, or at least acknowledge you being here?"

"Well we were__."

He never had a chance to finish his answer. We heard a quiet murmur from people in the room. Looking up, Veronica was being ushered in by a prison matron. She looked around at a few friendly faces- then focused on Joel and me, still issuing hateful looks. She didn't look at all attractive. Her eyes had dark circles around them, and her hair was without professional care. You could tell she was under extreme stress. She wore a casual light grey skirt and pearl- colored silk blouse with high heels to match. She was escorted to her defense attorney's table where she sat down.

Within a few minutes, the courtroom door opened, and the jury filed in- six men and six women with two female alternates. They took seats in the juror's box, then a loud voice from a court officer announced, "All rise. The Honorable Judge Thomas Markert presiding for The State of New Jersey."

As the judge entered the room, there was a slight pause. Quietness fell over the room. The demeanor the judge projected as he entered, resonated with the confidence in his years of legal jurisprudence.

Tall, in his mid to late 50's, he had a full head of graying hair, which added to his appearance of authority. After taking his seat, he remarked, "You may be seated."

"Miss. Ortega, is the district attorney's office ready to present your case?"

"Yes, Your Honor."

"Proceed."

Turning to the juror's box... "Ladies and gentleman of the jury, the case being presented to you today, is a murder that took place on Long Beach Island, in Beach Haven, New Jersey on the 8th of January, of this year." Continuing...

There are two defendants in this case that will be tried separately. It will be my duty as the District attorney, to connect the two defendants as being part of a crime that took the life of Heather O'Brien, a 22 year old from Ben Salem, Bucks County, Pennsylvania. My intention is to prove beyond a reasonable doubt, the defendant that you see before you, purposely and willingly lured the deceased to her shore home, where she participated in this violent act."

After her opening remarks, Judge Markert announced... "Miss Ortega, call your first witness."

"Will Ron Bennett, please take the stand." Rising from my seat, I took the witness stand and was sworn in.

"Mr. Bennett, would you tell us in your own words what took place on the night of January 8th of this year."

"I was on the beach at Beach Haven when I___" I was interrupted.

"Please tell the jury exactly where that is."

"It's a small community on the south end of Long Beach Island here in New Jersey."

"Go on- tell us what you observed that night."

I was walking the beach around ten 10 PM. When I crested the walkway from the beach, I observed two shadows on the closed drapes of the defendant's home." _I pointed to Veronica.

"When you say crested the walkway, exactly what does that mean? Would you clarify what a walkway is for the jury?"

Looking at the jury I said, "A walkway is a wooded bridge that goes over the sand dunes to access the beach."

"Thank you. Go on."

"And what exactly did you observe coming over the walkway?"

"I looked up at the defendant's picture window and saw the silhouette of a woman being strangled."

"Can you elaborate for the jury the actions of what the man did?"

"The man looked like he struck the woman on the side of the head with what appeared to be a vase or a lamp."

"Then what did you observe?"

"It looked like he bent down and picked the woman up by the neck and began strangling her."

The jury listened with great intent at my description. It was my turn to put all my journalistic descriptive skills to work, and I seized the moment. "Her arms seemed to be flailing- thrashing- and punching at the man. But it didn't seem to affect his death hold."

The defense rose to his feet. "Your Honor, I object to the witness' statement, 'Death hold.' That's something he couldn't have possibly known, whether she was actually dead or still alive."

"Objection sustained. You may strike the words 'death hold' from Mr. Bennett's testimony."

"Thank you, Your Honor."

"Miss Ortega, You may proceed."

"Mr. Bennett, Then what did you observe?"

"It looked like her arms were slowly losing strength, then they finally fell to her sides."

"What did you observe after that?"

"I hid on a patio next door and watched- thinking whoever did it wouldn't remain in the house very long."

"Did you see a body being removed?"

"Yes, it was placed in the trunk of an older model Chevy parked there- then driven away."

"And who did this?"

"It looked like a strong, stocky man who pretty much carried the body over his shoulder with ease."

"Then what did you do?"

"I stayed there waiting to see if he would return. I assumed he would."

"Why would you assume he would?"

"I didn't see another car outside so I assumed there had to be one in the garage."

"While you were waiting for his suspected return, did you see a female shadow on the drapes?"

"I saw what looked like a woman's shadow passing by the window."

The defense attorney rose to his feet. "Your Honor, I object. The district attorney's asking the witness to make a distinction as to the shadow on the drapes. On what basis does he have that determination?"

"Objection sustained. Council will not use a gender if it wasn't clearly defined."

"I apologize, your honor. Mr. Bennett, the silhouette you saw on the drapes after the body was removed, how would you describe it?"

"For the brief moment I observed it, it appeared considerably smaller than the man who carried the body away."

"What did you do then?"

"When another car came back and pulled into the driveway, I thought it may be someone else, possibly a visitor. When the man got out, I could see it was the same build as the man who put the body in the Chevy and drove away."

"In other words, it was a different car?"

"That's correct. It was a new Lincoln."

"What did you do then?"

"I ran down the beach to my own car, then went straight to the police station and told them what I saw."

"How long would you say you were there watching before summoning the police?"

"About 15 minutes."

"And you went straight to the police after leaving?"

"Yes."

"How much time would you say it took to get the police and return?"

"Probably another 15 minutes."

"And did you accompany the police to the defendant's house?"

"Yes, I described what I saw and pointed out the house where it took place."

"Then what happened?"

"Officer Ben Davis knocked at the door."

"Did the defendant answer it?"

"Yes, and she seemed to look shocked that I was there with the police."

The defense attorney quickly went to his feet, "Your Honor, I object to the witness' testimony that she looked shocked that he was there with the police at 10:00 or 10:30 at night- On a cold winter's night, I might add. Any normal person would be surprised by the visit by two police officers who weren't summoned."

"Objection sustained. Strike the word 'shocked' from the record."

"Thank you, Your Honor."

"Miss Ortega, You may continue."

"No more questions Your Honor."

"Mr. Denker, your witness."

Rising from his chair, he approached the witness stand. I could tell he seemed to remember my face, but I detected he couldn't recall the occasion. In his early 50's, he stood about 5 foot 10, balding, with a pale complexion. He wore a blue suit with a white shirt and what seemed to be a wide necktie that looked out of date. With his jacket unbuttoned, it exposed his somewhat portly frame.

"Thank you Your Honor. Mr. Bennett, let me try to understand something. You just happened to be walking the beach at 10 or 10:30 that night when you just happened to see this. Is that correct?"

"No, not exactly__ I was purposely going to the defendant's house."

"Why then, if you were purposely going to the defendants house, did you park two blocks away, then stealthily walk to her house from the darkness of the beach? Why didn't you just park out front and go to the house?"

"I wanted to warn the defendant of my meeting with her husband, and when I went by, there was another car there."

"What kind of car was that? Was it the defendant's?"

"No, it was an older model Chevrolet."

"Then the defendant's car wasn't there?"

"Not parked outside, but I assumed__." I was cut short.

Raising his voice, Mr. Denker said- "Mr. Bennett, I don't want an assumption. All the court wants to know is what you observed. Did you or did you not see the defendant's car?"

"No, I didn't."

"You say you were purposely going to the house. Why would you continue going to the defendant's house if you didn't see her car?"

"I thought it may have been in the garage."

"Seeing the older Chevy, did you assume her husband's car was in the garage?"

"Yes."

"Did you see the defendant's car at all that night?"

"Yes, after everything happened and Officer Davis and I went back to the house, I saw it in the garage."

"In other words, you never saw it until after she was taken into custody."

"That's correct."

"Is it possible that the defendant wasn't there at all, but came between the time you observed the shadows on the drapes and the time you returned with the police?"

"Objection, Your Honor. Council's trying to suggest the witness not seeing the defendant's car, excuses her from being at the scene."

"Sorry Your Honor- Mr. Bennett, what made you believe the defendant was in danger for her life? Was it some sort of premonition?"

"I was led to believe by Mrs. Simmons at the time, her husband was- or may have been- the person who killed his secretary. She said she was afraid he was planning to kill the current one, and I thought his car was parked in the garage. That's the first thought that entered my mind when I saw the scene on the closed drapes."

"But it wasn't, was it?"

"No, after the body was removed and put in the trunk of the Chevy, the person left, then returned a short time later, in a Lincoln."

"Then at no time did you see the defendant's car?"

"Not until after she was taken into custody and went back with Officer Davis."

"Tell me, the defendant's husband called you and asked if you would meet him at a sports bar on City Line Avenue in Philadelphia. Is that correct?"

"Yes, that's correct."

"And would you tell the court what Mr. Simmons asked you at that meeting?"

I looked over at Joel, realizing he was helping Veronica, and knew I could only answer that question one way. "He asked me not to try and contact his wife again."

"So the meeting was about you possibly having a secret affair with his wife? How many times have you secretly contacted or attempted to contact the defendant?"

Miss Ortega's rose to her feet. "I object Your Honor. The meaning of 'attempt' isn't exactly how many times he actually contacted the defendant. He may have attempted 10 times but was only successful at reaching her once."

"Objection sustained- Mr. Denker, refrain from using the word 'attempt' and use the language of actually contacting the defendant."

"Thank you, Your Honor. Mr. Bennett, let me rephrase that question. How many times would you say you actually had contact with the defendant?"

Pausing to think, I began to relate my thoughts in words- words loud enough to tell the jury my inner thoughts. "Well let's see- the day I discovered the body on the beach, when she let me use her phone to call the police. The next time I saw her was about a week later. She was walking the beach and saw me fishing, and stopped to tell me about her personal problems with her husband."

Quickly interrupting my testimony, Mr. Denker asked, "And what were her problems with her husband?"

"She told me about the argument with her husband, and told me he was coming to the shore, and she didn't want to be there when he arrived. Then another time when she left the note under my windshield wiper__."

My testimony was stopped again. "You don't have to reveal the circumstances, just how many times?"

"Possibly 10- Let's see, yes about 10, I would say."

I knew I threw him a curve with his line of questioning, but it was only a brief detour.

"The personal meetings you had, were any of them amorous?"

I couldn't deny it, and didn't want to perjure myself. "Yes, with seeing her distraught time after time over her home life, I became interested in her."

"In other words, you were taking advantage of a troubled woman?"

I tried to recover. He was making me look like a vulture preying on an innocent person__ anything but the actual truth.

"No, I was taken in by her charm and innuendos of trying to get away from an abusive husband and a bad situation. She seemed trapped. She explained to me on several occasions how her husband was emotionally tough to live with- even physically abusive on a few occasions- something she could no longer tolerate. I didn't want anything happening to her, so it became more of a concern for her safety. I even took her to the police station for an interview about her husband's abuse. Later on, it became an interest in possibly having a relationship with her."

"What do you mean concern for her safety?"

"She told me about the wild changes in her husband's character. He was jealous, as she put it, extremely jealous. At the meeting with her husband, he showed me a dossier by a private detective on Veronica. I believe I was one of several__" Cutting me off abruptly, Mr. Denker said, "You said you took her to the police station. Do you know whether there was a complaint filed?"

"I don't think so, not at that time."

"I take it you drove her to the police station? I assume it was from Philadelphia. Did you go straight back to the city after the interview?"

Again, I couldn't get around it. I was trapped. "No, we stopped at a restaurant to have lunch on the way back."

"Do you remember what restaurant that was?"

"Yes, it was Claxton's Log Cabin."

"What did you talk about over lunch?"

"I was beginning to get more and more worried about her staying with her husband."

"Did you have an argument over it?"

"I wouldn't call it an argument. I__"

I was cut short again "Well, when you raised your voice at the defendant, didn't the waitress have to come to the table and ask what was wrong? In fact, she had to come to the table twice. Isn't that correct?"

"Yes, but it wasn't an argument. I was just loudly adamant, stating my concern for her."

"Isn't it true that it was really over you wanting her to leave her husband, and she didn't want to do it?"

"Like I said counselor, it was only for her own safety that I was concerned."

Sporadically during my questioning, the jury began to murmur.

"Mr. Bennett, Isn't it true that you surprised the defendant with a visit around 10 o'clock one evening?"

"Yes."

"What was her response?"

"She was surprised to see me. That's when I told her about the meeting with her husband."

"That was the middle of December, correct?"

"Yes, around then."

"How long did you stay? I assume it was cold. Were you invited to stay the night?"

"No, it was a short visit. After I told her about the meeting with her husband, she told me I should leave. She wanted to think things over, about how she was going to leave him."

Raising his voice in a tone that was lashing at me, he said. "So she more or less, as you're describing the argument at the restaurant, was about leaving her husband, and not inviting you to stay for the night. I guess it's safe to assume she didn't really want a relationship with you at all, and was politely fighting your advances. Is that correct?"

Miss Ortega rose to her feet once again. "Your Honor, I object. Council is assuming a lot of the witness' good intentions are somehow connected to the events of the night in question and therefore irrelevant."

"Your Honor, it has everything to do with my next line of questioning."

"Objection overruled. Continue with your questioning, Mr. Denker."

"Thank you, Your Honor. Mr. Bennett, you're a reporter, are you not?"

"Yes, I'm a freelance investigative reporter."

Smiling gaining my confidence he said... "I've read some of your stories. They're pretty thorough. I believe you won several journalism prizes, is that correct?"

"Yes, that's correct."

"Would you say your stories tend to lean toward the sensationalist slant?"

"No counselor. I write them as I see them- or rather, where my investigation takes me. I have no control over the events."

A murmur came up from the jury box, and one of the jurors leaned to the juror on his right, quietly saying, "I thought I recognized him. He's a good reporter."

The judge, hearing the comment, looked in the jury's direction, banging his gavel. "The jurors will refrain from further conversation... Continue Mr. Denker."

"Your Honor, I just wanted to point out to the jury- The witness, in his exuberance to report a story, given the chance, wouldn't he much rather report a sensational story?"

Miss Ortega immediately stood... "Your Honor, I object. Council is attacking the integrity of the witness' proven professionalism. He's not the one on trial here."

"Objection sustained." The judge pointed to the court stenographer. "Have that last remark stricken from the record." Turning to Mr. Denker... "Counselor, I see no reason for you to attack a person who's proved himself without reproach in his field. Continue with this case."

"I only have a few more questions, Your Honor. Mr. Bennett, when you drove past the defendant's and saw an older car, did you assume Mr. Simmons car was in the garage."

"Yes."

"Why did you park two blocks away? Why not one block? -Or at the end of the street? You testified you saw the silhouettes of a woman being strangled by a man and you did nothing! Why didn't you just bang on the front door and maybe avoid her being murdered?"

I was taken by surprise and was beginning to fumble for words- me, a reporter. What was he up to? What line of questioning was he pursuing?

"I guess I was taken by surprise, it all happened so quickly. For a second I wasn't sure of what I was witnessing was real. I really can't answer that question accurately."

"Then let me try to understand something. You say you were in fear for the defendant's life, but you didn't take steps to maybe thwart a woman being murdered. Could it be there was some other reason? Could it be that if it was Mr. Simmons strangling a woman, it would remove him as an obstacle between you and the defendant?"

The courtroom erupted in gasps and comments to one another.

"No! No! That's not it at all." I was beginning to get upset at his accusations.

Miss Ortega rose. "I object, Your Honor. Again, the defense is try-ing to discredit the witness' testimony. He's not the one on trial."

"Mr. Denker, you've been warned to keep away from hypotheti-cals, I don't need to remind you again, do I?"

"No, Your Honor. Mr. Bennett, you said you only saw a brief shadow passing behind the drapes after the body was removed. At that time, you were still watching the male putting the body in the trunk outside. Is that correct?

"Yes."

"Then you couldn't definitely identify the defendant as the person you saw?"

"That's correct."

"You stated your actions, along with the time it took for the police to arrive, and finally get to the front door, was approximately 15 minutes. Is that correct?"

"Yes, that's correct."

Let's go over it again. You testified you watched for about 10 minutes after the body was removed. Correct?"

"Yes, that's correct."

"You then stated you ran down the beach and drove to the police station- How long did that take?"

"I'd say about 10 minutes, maybe a little longer."

"After you told Officer Davis what you saw, you went with him to the intersection and waited for another patrol car. Isn't that correct?"

"Yes, we waited for Officer Kevin Jones to arrive."

"And how long did it take Officer Jones to get where you were?"

"About 10 minutes."

"Then let's add these times together. Fifteen minutes between the time the body was removed and the Lincoln returned. Another 15 minutes to get to your car and get to the police station. Ten minutes to tell Officer Davis and get to the intersection where you waited for Officer Jones. Another 10 minute wait- until he arrived. How long were they talking strategy before they knocked at the door?"

"I'd say another 5 minutes."

"Let's see, that adds up to be around, 45 or 50 minutes- and not 10 or 15 minutes as you testified. When you were asked to add all the events together it comes to a bare minimum of 40 minutes. Which figure is more accurate?"

"I guess thirty five or forty minutes would be more accurate."

"You thought it was not unusual to park two blocks away? Could it be that the defendant also parked away from the house, thinking that was her husband's secretary's car, and arrived between the time you were there, and the time you returned with the police?"

"It's possible, but__" …I was cut short.

"No further questions, Your Honor."

"Miss Ortega- If you have no further questions, call your next witness."

"Thank you, Your Honor. I call Officer Ben Davis to the stand."

"Officer Ben Davis, please take the witness stand."

After being sworn in, Miss Ortega began the questioning.

"Officer Davis: On the night in question, what was your recollection of the events that took place?"

"If it pleases the court Your Honor, I was on duty at the police department office."

"And what took place?"

"At about 10 o'clock Mr. Bennett knocked at the door- then came into the office."

"And did he come in the office as a matter of fact, slow and calm, as if it was a friendly visit?"

"No, he was very excited. I'd say almost to the point where he had a hard time relaying what he just witnessed."

"And what did he say he witnessed?"

"He said he saw shadows on the drapes of a house where he saw a man striking a woman on the side of the head, then pick her up off the floor by the neck and strangle her."

"What else did he tell you?"

"He said the man carried the body out of the house and put it in the trunk of a car, then drove away."

"Did he tell you anything else he observed?"

"Yes, after we left the office and were in route to the house, he said he saw what looked like a shadow of a woman still in the house."

"And what did he tell you the woman was doing?"

"He said it looked like she was attempting to straighten up the room."

"And what did he tell you about how the shadow was straightening up the room?"

Mr. Denker jumped to his feet. "Your Honor, I object to council's term, 'What she might be doing.' First of all, Mr. Bennett said he only observed the silhouette for a few seconds go by the window. How could he know exactly what the shadow was doing?"

"Objection sustained. Miss Ortega, we're interested in what Mr. Bennett actually saw, not suppositions or imaginary facts."

"My apology- Your Honor."

"Did Mr. Bennett tell you anything else he observed that evening?"

"No. When Officer Jones arrived at the location, we discussed our strategy as to how we were going to confront the occupants after knocking at the door."

"After you knocked, what happened?"

"Mrs. Simmons answered the door."

"Was Mr. Bennett there?"

"Yes, he was standing behind Officer Jones and me."

"What was the look on the defendant's face? Was she shocked? Did she look surprised at Mr. Bennett's presence?"

"She didn't see him at first and seemed surprised. She stood looking at us for a few seconds, trying to understand why we were there. When she saw Mr. Bennett, her face went from being surprised to being shocked. Then a completely blank look."

"Your Honor, I object to the validity of facial expressions by the defendant. As I said before, anyone confronted by a knock on the door at that late hour, only to open it and see not just one, but two policeman at the door who weren't summoned, anyone would be surprised. That would be a normal reaction for any rational person."

"The court recognizes Mr. Denker's statement. It wouldn't be out of the ordinary. You may proceed Miss Ortega."

"Officer Davis, I understand you're the author of a book. Is that correct?"

"Yes."

"Please tell the jury the title of that book and when it was written."

Turning to face the jury- "I wrote it almost two years ago. I titled it, "The Face Tells it All.""

"And please tell us what that book is about."

"It's a study I began almost 20 years ago. It deals with my experiences of studying facial expressions by people I had contact with over the years in various situations."

"And what exactly do you mean by facial expressions?"

"When people are confronted with authority- how they react, whether it's a crime committed, a traffic stop, domestic disturbance or an auto accident- they have a variety of facial expressions."

"And where in that category would you say the defendant's facial expression was."

"According to my experiences, more shock than surprise. When she saw Mr. Bennett standing with us, her expression went from shock to embarrassment, then to an almost controlled anger."

"You say embarrassed. What do you mean by that?"

"Her face turned red when she saw Officer Jones and me, but when she saw Mr. Bennett, it contorted to a sneer, extremely nervous, a very controlled anger, as if his concern for her safety wasn't welcomed."

The jury murmured again, impressed as I was with his description. I sat back in my seat, surprised at his ability to catalog in his mind, her every expression. Thinking about it, he was exceptionally descriptive. He described it to a T.

"Officer Davis, do you remember exactly what was said by the defendant?"

Taking a notebook from his pocket, Ben said, "I'll read the exact exchange of words between them. The defendant said, 'Why Ron,' referring to Mr. Bennett, 'Were you so afraid for my safety you had to bring a whole army of police?' Mr. Bennett then replied to that statement. 'Is that all you can say after what I witnessed?'

"Then what happened, Officer Davis?"

"I asked if there was anyone else in the house."

"And was there?"

"Yes, that's when Carl Dunn came down the stairs."

"What did you do then?"

"I took Mr. Dunn and Mrs. Simmons into custody, and brought them back to the police station."

"Did you take them both in the same vehicle?"

"No, I separated them. Officer Jones took Mr. Dunn, and I drove Mrs. Simmons along with Mr. Bennett back."

"Did Mrs. Simmons say anything on the way back to the station?"

"No, I advised her not to say anything until I read her the Miranda Rights. We hadn't recovered the body yet."

"What did you do after you arrived at the police station?"

"When we arrived, Officer Jones was already there, and I instructed him to take Mr. Dunn into another office while I interviewed Mr. Bennett."

"Where was the defendant at the time?"

"She was sitting at another desk in the same room."

"Go on. Then what happened?"

"She seemed to be very annoyed at Mr. Bennett's recount of the night, but didn't say anything directly to him. About halfway through his interview, Officer Jones stepped out of the inner office, where he was with Mr. Dunn. He told me Mr. Dunn wanted to speak to me in private."

"And what was that about?"

"We stepped out into the hallway, and he informed me that Mr. Dunn wanted to confess."

"Then what happened?"

"I brought Mr. Dunn into the room where I was interviewing Mr. Bennett, and Officer Jones took Mrs. Simmons into the other room."

"Was anything said during the changing of rooms between the defendant and Mr. Dunn?"

Taking out his notebook again, he said, "Yes, as they passed each other in the office, she said, "You stupid bastard__" He was interrupted.

Mr. Denker quickly rose to his feet. "Your Honor, what transpired between them under these tense circumstances is irrelevant. It has no bearing on the defendant's guilt or innocence."

Miss Ortega interjected__ "On the contrary your honor... it's all part of showing the jury the defendant's distain for someone caught up in the same unfortunate situation and her slanderous remark about the low intelligence level of Mr. Dunn."

"Objection overruled, you may proceed Miss. Ortega."

"Again, Officer Davis, what were the exact words of the defendant when she passed Mr. Dunn in your office?"

Reading from his note pad, he said, "I should have known better than to get involved with a stupid bastard like you."

The jury and spectators looked at each other and began to mumble again at the statement.

Judge Markert banged his gavel once again. "Order in the court:"

"What did you do then?"

"I discontinued Mr. Bennett's statement and immediately read Mr. Dunn his Miranda Rights, then took a full confession from him."

"And how far back did that confession go with a personal relationship between the defendant and Mr. Dunn?"

Mr. Denker rose... "I object, Your Honor. A confession from a co-defendant has no real validity. There's no way to separate truth from fiction."

"Objection sustained. Miss. Ortega, re-phrase your question."

"Certainly Your Honor. Officer Davis, did he tell you when their earliest encounter- personally or professionally- took place?"

"Your Honor please, Council is still trying to bring to light- an affair that may have never even happened. That's only conjecture from the co-defendant."

"Objection sustained. Council will discontinue the assumption that there was a relationship at the early stages of their meetings."

"Officer Davis, did Mr. Dunn tell you when he and the Simmons' first came together?"

"Yes, it was when Mr. Dunn began going over the plans for the house the defendant and her husband wanted him to build. He was the contractor they selected."

"The relationship culminated with the events when you took them both into custody. Is that correct?"

"Yes, I believe so."

"Officer, on the night in question, did you go back to the Simmons home?"

"Yes, I did."

"Tell the jury what took place."

"After I took Mr. Dunn's statement, Mr. Simmons arrived at the police station. He was summoned by Mr. Bennett. I told him I needed to secure a warrant to search his premises, and he told me it wasn't necessary. He would sign a waiver and go with me. In fact, he offered me a key and told me I could go in whenever I thought it was necessary."

"And did he go with you?"

"Yes, he unlocked the door and stayed the whole time I was searching and taking photos."

"Please describe for the jury the scene of the crime."

Turning to the jury Ben began, "The living room is on the second floor, as with most of the newer sea shore homes. The ground level is primarily parking area and a garage. It's built that way to minimize storm damage in case of flooding. The top of the stairs is the actual entry point of the living room it's divided by two large white sectional sofas.

A chromed- base glass coffee table is in the center with matching glass end tables, and white shaded light gray based ceramic lamps on each. One of the lamp shades was twisted out of shape, and its base had a slight crack. There was a large dirt spot on the carpet from what looked like a tropical plant pot on a pedestal. The pot that held the plant was only half full, and the plant wasn't solidly anchored in the remaining soil. There's a bar against the wall in the far end of the room."

"Will you describe for the jury the bar area."

"The bar is walnut with a black leather front, and gray- covered chrome stools that match the carpeting. A wine glass rack and bottle holder is on the wall just behind the bar."

"Did you have a chance to search the bar area?"

"Yes, I took several glasses from the bar and placed them in plastic evidence bags. I made notations as to where I retrieved them and I took photos of where they were before I removed them."

"With the analysis of the glasses were the defendants finger prints present on any of them?"

"No: only the deceased, Carl Dunn's and Mr. Simmons'."

"What else did you retrieve from the bar?"

"I removed three glasses from a small dishwasher behind the bar and a small blue bottle from one of the drawers. it was described to me in Mr. Dunn's statement as the bottle__…"

"I object your honor… Again the statement from the co-defendant is totally biased and irrelevant."

"Objection sustained. Council will not refer to a co-defendants' statement' only what the officer actually did. Proceed."

"Officer Davis, you retrieved a small blue bottle from a drawer at the bar. Describe for the jury what the bottle looked like."

"It was a small blue bottle with a rubber stopper. The kind you could draw up a measured amount from, and dispense it by the drop. I held it up to the light and saw it was almost empty. There were visible fingerprints on it, and I put it a plastic evidence bag also."

"Do you know what was in the bottle?"

"I object, Your Honor. The officer isn't a chemical analyst."

Miss Ortega snapped back. "He isn't, Your Honor, but I have the chemical analysis from the State Police Chemical Lab. I can read it for the jury if the defense council would like."

"Mr. Denker, I don't think it would be out of line for the officer to speak about an official document from the chemical lab do you?"

"No, Your Honor. My apology;"

"And what was the chemical analysis of the bottle?" Miss Ortega handed Ben the report.

"The analysis came back as chloral hydrate."

The court stenographer responded, "Excuse me, what was that chemical analysis?"

"Chloral hydrate- Spelled, *CHLORAL HYDRATE.*"

"Thank you. Sorry for the interruption Your Honor."

Miss Ortega proceeded. "And did the analysis say what it was used for?"

"The medical examiner told me it was used for insomniacs and as a relaxer prior to surgeries."

"And what other effects did it have?"

"An overdose would put a person in a near comatose state and render them pretty much defenseless__..."

"I object Your Honor. I request the last remarks from the witness be stricken from the record. Is he merely stating personal opinion or what was officially written in a report- a report, I might add, that council failed to provide to the defense."

Miss Ortega rose from her chair and walked across the room showing Judge Merkert the chemical analysis. After the judge looked at it, he instructed Miss Ortega to show it to Mr. Denker. After examining it, he handed it back.

Judge Markert remarked, "Is the defense satisfied with the validity of the coroner's report?"

"Yes, Your Honor. Thank you."

"Miss Ortega, you may proceed."

"And what did the Coroner relate to you?"

"He said an overdose would render the person indefensible, if not fatal."

"You said you retrieved a few glasses from the dishwasher. Were their fingerprints on them?"

"Yes."

"How many and whose prints were on them?"

"There were some prints of the defendant and her husband on one, and Mr. Simmons and the deceased on another. There were also two glasses that had only Mr. Simmons and Carl Dunn's prints on them."

"Anything else you can tell us?"

"Yes on one of the glasses was a lipstick mark- the same color the defendant was wearing when she was taken into custody. There was also a chemical analysis of the residue in the glasses."

"And what did that analysis reveal?"

"One glass had Mr. Simmons' and Mrs. Simmons' fingerprints on it. The chemical analysis of the contents revealed a special Chablis wine. I also retrieved an empty bottle from the trash can that was the same vintage."

"I object, Your Honor. Chablis is a common wine used by millions. It happens to be my favorite also."

"Officer: what can you tell us about the Chablis in question? Is it as common as the defense would lead us to believe?"

"No Your Honor, the chemical analysis said it's a Chablis__" Taking his notebook from his pocket once again... "Your Honor, it's called Domaine Francois Raveneau Chablis Burgundy- the same as the empty bottle that was in the trash can."

Miss Ortega replied to the description. "Sounds pretty expensive and not the common liquor store variety, as the defense suggests."

"According to the wine store I checked with, it sells for a $108 dollars a bottle."

"And what, if anything, did that other glass have in it?"

"The same vintage as the Chablis Wine from the bottle I retrieved from the trash can, with a trace of chloral hydrate in it."

"And whose fingerprints were on that glass?"

"The deceased, the defendants, and Mr. Simmons' prints."

"And whose fingerprints were on the empty bottle?"

"The defendant's:"

"Then, in your opinion, if the defendant's husband had his prints on them, wouldn't it be safe to say he went to the house before he went to the police station?"

"I would say so."

"You say there were two other glasses with Mr. Simmons' and Carl Dunn's prints. Were those glasses also examined for content?"

"Yes, the analysis revealed they contained scotch- a diluted scotch, and the chem. lab thought they might have been scotch and water or just scotch with melted ice. At any rate, the scotch was diluted."

"You were at the scene when the body was recovered. Explain to the court what you observed."

"The body was a young girl partially wrapped in a blanket- tall with long blond hair, approximately 25. After removing the blanket- she was completely naked. She had a gash on the left side of her head with what appeared to be dry blood surrounding it. There were also bruises around the neck and chest area."

"What did the analysis say of what was in her stomach at the time of her death?"

"The same type of wine with a trace of chloral hydrate."

A murmur came from the spectators, and Judge Markert had to restore order.

"How far away from the Simmons' home was it?"

"About half a mile."

"Was there a car of the deceased recovered?"

"Yes, it was about two blocks from where the deceased was dumped."

"Was there any evidence of the body being transported in it?"

"Yes, there were blood stains in the trunk that matched the deceased and a few blond hairs."

"So with Mr. Bennett's testimony- the co-defendant carrying the body out of the house and placing it in the trunk of the decedent's car, then returning in his own- would lead you to believe it was pre- planned. Isn't that correct?"

"Yes, it would seem so. The co-defendants car had to be within the same area that was planned to dump the body."

"I object, Your Honor. The officer's testimony is an assumption."

Miss Ortega responded, "On the contrary Your Honor, the case for premeditation is more than an assumption- It wouldn't be beyond reason, that the murder was planned, right down to where the co-defendants' car was already parked.

It was within close proximity of where they intended to dispose of the body. According to Mr. Bennett's testimony, he waited on the patio of the residence next door, and after about 10 minutes, the co-defendant returned- not in the car of the deceased that drove away, but in the car that was later identified as the car belonging to Mr. Dunn. The very same car she lied about, that led Mr. Bennett to believe belonged to her abusive husband."

"Objection overruled. It would certainly seem like it, if the time span was that short and the distance was that far. Assuming it would take about that much time or even longer, wouldn't be out of the question."

"Miss Ortega, you may proceed."

"Officer, tell the jury once again, what else did the coroner's report have to say about the cause of death?"

"The forensic report said she had an overdose of chloral hydrate in her system but died from strangulation. She also had a slight fracture from blunt trauma to the left side of her temple."

Again the room was abuzz from the spectators. Joel going to the house before getting to the police station told me he was trying to hide evidence and once again the judge had to restore silence.

"Miss Ortega, do you have any further questions?"

"Just one more, Your Honor..."

"Officer, did you receive photographs from the Woman's Detention Center after Mrs. Simmons was taken there?"

"Yes."

"And what did the photographs show?"

"There were signs of bruises beginning to appear on the defendant's neck and arms."

Taking the pictures from her case folder, Miss Ortega showed them to the judge before getting permission to pass them to the jury.

"You may proceed, Miss Ortega."

"Thank you Your Honor."

Handing them to the jury, they passed them to each other before returning them to the district attorney.

"Mr. Denker, your witness."

"Officer Davis, you testified that Mr. Simmons returned with you to the house. Was there anything different from the first time you went there when you initially confronted the defendant and Mr. Dunn?"

"Not that I could see, no."

"You testified you took some glasses and a small blue bottle that contained chloral hydrate for fingerprints. What were the results of those tests?"

"The glasses from the coffee table only had the fingerprints of Mr. Dunn and Mr. Simmons on them. Another glass had the deceased fingerprints."

"Was the defendant's prints on any of those glasses?

"No."

"Were there any prints on the chloral hydrate bottle?"

"Yes."

"Who's fingerprints were on the bottle?"

"The prints were the defendant's husbands and a partially smudged print that couldn't be identified."

"Then how do you account for the confession of Mr. Dunn saying the defendant was the one he saw putting the drops in the deceased glass?"

"I can't account for that. The only identifiable prints on the bottle belonged to Mr. Simmons."

"Well, how was it that Mr. Simmons' prints were on the bottle when he was in Philadelphia at the time of the murder and the co-defendant said he saw Mrs. Simmons use that same bottle to put the chloral hydrate in the deceased's drink, only a few hours before?"

"I can't answer that, unless he went to the house before coming to the police station that night. That would be the only way."

"Then without the defendant's fingerprints or even knowing whether she was at the house at the time of the murder, it's quite possible that she's a victim of circumstance, isn't that correct."

Miss Ortega... "I object Your Honor. It's not for the officer to determine this case but the sole responsibility of the jury."

"Objection sustained. Council will refrain from having the witness render a decision on the innocence or guilt of the defendant. Proceed with the case."

"My apology- Your Honor. Officer Davis, you testified that there was a broken lamp with a twisted shade. Approximately how large was the base of that lamp?"

"About six inches around, maybe a little bigger."

"If that's the case, it would take a pretty big hand to pick it up and hold it, let alone swing it at a person violently, would it not?"

"I would say that."

"Well, in view of Mr. Bennett's testimony, the defendant couldn't have possibly been mistaken for Mr. Dunn."

"No, he never said in his statement it was anyone else but a man figure."

"Then at best the charge should be, is being an accessory after the fact, and aiding in the disposing of a body, if in fact, she was there at all."

"I object, Your Honor. The police department only presents evidence to the District Attorney's Office of the incident as they record it. The district attorney decides the charges."

"Defense will not imply the police department has sole responsibility of the charges leveled against the defendant."

"No further questions your honor."

Miss Ortega stood... "Your Honor, just one more question for the witness. Did Mr. Simmons at any time say he went to the house before he got to the police station?"

"No, he said he came straight there."

"Then he could possibly be lying and did go there first, and wipe the chloral hydrate bottle clean, of the defendants prints. In fact, he could have destroyed any evidence of the defendant being there at all, isn't that correct?"

"Yes, that's true. From what Mr. Dunn confessed, he would have___" He was cut short.

"I object, Your Honor. Prosecution can only state an opinion of whether he went there and not elaborate on what Mr. Simmons might have done."

"Objection sustained."

"Officer Davis, you're friends with the co-defendant, isn't that correct?"

"Yes, we're both islanders. We've known each other since kindergarten."

"That's quite some time. Your book on facial expressions was very interesting to say the least, very impressive. How would you describe Mr. Dunn's face when he came to the door?"

"His initial facial expression was complete dismay. He looked very dejected."

"Can you expand on the term dejected?"

"He had the expression of someone trapped in a situation from which there was no escape."

"Thank you. No further questions Your Honor."

After hearing his testimony, I realized that's exactly what had to have happened. I remember that evening when I stood in the doorway with Ben and Kevin, I could see past Veronica. I remember I noticed some dirt from the flower pot still on the floor. They never had a chance to go back and pick it up. He had to have gone there first. That's why the concern about the district attorney taking me out to the hallway before the proceedings began.

It wasn't looking very good for Carl. He was self confessed, and there was no way legally to tie Veronica up with the murders. There wasn't much physical evidence, or it didn't seem so.

Judge Markert remarked, "Miss Ortega, call your next witness."

"Your Honor- it's already after 12. My next witness will take at least an hour. If your honor could call the lunch break a little sooner than the normal, council would greatly appreciate it."

"Mr. Denker, do you have any objection?"

"No, Your Honor."

"This court stands adjourned until 1:30."

Court officer in a loud voice said, "All rise while the judge retires to chamber."

Chapter 10

Exiting the room, I thought it was necessary to ask, "Miss Ortega, is there going to be a surprise witness?"

"Mr. Bennett, You'll find out at 1:30."

Through lunch, I wondered what the district attorney had in mind, and was anxious to get back to the courtroom. With everyone seated, the judge re-entered the room.

"Miss Ortega, Call your next witness."

"Thank you, Your Honor. Will Mr. Joel Simmons please take the stand:"

Anticipating the request, he cast an eye toward Veronica and her defense attorney. Hesitantly, he rose from his seat and slowly walked to the witness box. After being sworn in- he sat down.

"Mr. Simmons, do you recall the night you were summoned to the police station? The night Mrs. Simmons was arrested?"

"Yes."

"Do you remember being interviewed by Policeman Davis?"

"Yes."

"Isn't it true that in your interview you told Officer Davis about your wife's obsession trying to appear young?"

"Your Honor, I object. I think everyone tries to present themselves in the best possible light."

"Miss Ortega, Where's your line of questioning leading?"

"Your Honor, my intention is to bring out an overly obsessed mind- a mind that could give cause to the defendant's action."

"Objection overruled, you may continue."

"Thank you, Your Honor."

"Now then, Mr. Simmons- in your interview, you told Officer Davis about the great lengths the defendant, your wife, would take trying to stave off the appearance of aging. Isn't that correct?"

"Yes, but don't most women?"

"Thank you for the comment, but I'm the one asking the questions. During that interview, you even mentioned the expense of her going to different doctors exploring different facial treatments. Isn't that true?"

Looking at Veronica he hesitated to answer- then finally said, "Yes, every married man should try to support his wife's attempt to do what makes them happy? You don't think that some balding men don't worry about their wife remaining attracted to them?"

"Well isn't it true that in the defendant's case it became an over-whelming insecurity, and she would lash out at you unprovoked about the young age of secretaries you hired? Isn't that true, Mr. Simmons?"

Joel sympathetically looked at Veronica- then looked down at the floor. "Yes, she did have some hang- ups about the aging process."

"How recent- the last six months, the last year- just how long?"

"The accusations started when she hit her 30th birthday, maybe a little later."

"Well, that's been at least six or seven years ago. By that statement, I take it the older she got, the worse the problem became. Is that true?"

Casting an eye at Veronica again- then looking down at the floor, he hesitantly answered, "Yes, that's true, but such insecurities are not uncommon."

"During your meeting at the sports bar with Mr. Bennett, did you mention any of this to him?"

"No. Why would that be any of his business, I just asked him to refrain from calling- or seeing- my wife."

"Well, didn't your paranoia with your wife's actions and the fact you thought she may be having an extra marital affair, cause you to hire a private detective to follow her?"

"Yes:"

"As you stated- when the problems got worse- instead of having her followed, why didn't you suggest to your wife she should consult a psychiatrist or psychologist for professional help?"

"I thought I could help her myself. I kept trying to make her feel more secure by complimenting her, taking her out to dinner, buying her flowers and occasionally buying her a piece of jewelry for no special occasion."

Mr. Denker quickly rose to his feet. "I object, Your Honor. The witness lacks the professional ability to diagnose the defendant. Council's suggesting the defendant's mental problems have something to do with the charges the defendant's facing today."

Miss Ortega responded… "Your Honor, I can think of no better person to identify erratic behavior than one's spouse just by their daily contact."

"Objection overruled. You may continue."

"Now then, did you ever suggest that?"

"No!"

"In your interview with Officer Davis, you mentioned hiring your secretaries from a temp service, is that correct?"

Judge Markert asked, "Miss Ortega- If you would clarify for the jury what the term temp secretary' refers to."

"Certainly Your Honor." Turning to the jury- "The term temp is the short- term for temporary."

"Thank you Miss Ortega, you may continue."

"When you hire short- term secretaries or temps, as you call them- Generally how long is their tenure?"

"Some last six months, some last longer. It depends on the amount of work at the time and their efficiency."

"In your statement to Officer Davis, you said there were several who only lasted a few months. Do you recall any of them?"

"Yes, the first one who abruptly quit was a little over a year ago."

"And the next one, when was that?"

"That was about nine months ago."

"What is your pay scale in comparison to other companies that hire temps?"

"I'd say we were the upper echelon pay scale."

"Then to your estimation there would be no real reason for them to just suddenly quit?"

"I object, Your Honor. They're any number of reasons a person may quit a job. If the inference is somehow trying to focus on my client as the cause, it's strictly hypothetical."

"Objection sustained. Unless Miss Ortega, there's a purpose in connecting the witness to the defendant."

"There is in this case Your Honor, if I may be allowed to continue."

"Proceed."

"Mr. Simmons, these two secretaries who suddenly and without prior notice quit- to your recollection, were they efficient in their duties?"

"Yes, I would say so."

"Then if your pay scale was superior, why wouldn't you question their employer?"

"I never thought to ask. They just sent another replacement."

"That's what you told Officer Davis during his interview, but the truth of the matter is, you lied. I telephoned the company and spoke to a woman who's in charge of placing the temps- a Mrs. Makin. She told me she places the girls according to the firm's needs and the temps. qualifications. She said she personally contacted your office and asked about their sudden disappearance without a response. In Mr. Bennett's statement, he mentioned the defendant telling him about a private detective calling her, asking about a missing girl. Were you aware of that?"

Joel's face was beginning to show signs of embarrassment and shot back with a quick, "No."

"There was a body of a temp secretary discovered buried in the sand dunes about a hundred yards from your house by Mr. Bennett. Did you know her?"

A muffled murmur came from the spectators. Judge Markert announced, "Order in the court."

Pounding a clenched fist on the panel separating the jury from the room, in a raised voice, Miss. Ortega demanded, "Mr. Simmons! I ask you again: did you know the deceased?"

"Yes, I did."

"Was she a temp from your office?"

"Yes, she was at first, but I liked her work and put her on the permanent payroll."

"And how long had she been with the company?"

"About six or seven months."

"Did you know her name?"

"Yes, I believe her name was Karen White."

Miss Ortega shot back. "*Believe* her name was Karen White?" She repeated, "*Believe* her name was Karen White. The truth is- you *knew* her name. Weren't you having an affair with her?"

Looking tense, he replied, "Yes, it started out as an affair, but we became engaged after I realized my marital problems with Mrs. Simmons couldn't be resolved."

"When Karen's body was discovered, she was wearing a ring- an engagement ring with the initials J.S. to K.W. with Love! You knew her, yet you didn't come forward to tell the authorities who she was or how you were connected. Is it because you had an idea- your wife may have had a hand in her demise?"

"I object Your Honor. Council's putting words in the witness' mouth. The defendant's not on trial for the death of Mr. Simmons' fiancée."

"Objection sustained. Miss Ortega, confine your questions to the trial at hand."

"Sorry Your Honor. Mr. Simmons, Why didn't you tell the authorities? You must have had a reason. It's not like she was just an employee. She was someone you were about to be devoted to for the rest of your life."

"I was afraid I might have been a suspect. Our engagement was between the two of us. No one else knew- not even her parents."

"The chemical analysis of her autopsy revealed she had chloral hydrate in her system also- the same substance as the deceased that the defendant's being accused of today. A substance in a bottle recovered from a drawer behind the bar at your shore home with your finger prints on it. How do you account for that?"

"I can't. Maybe I inadvertently moved the bottle looking through the drawer for something."

Joel looked at Veronica. Did he just transfer the blame to himself for Karen White's murder?

"You say you never suggested the defendant seek professional help for her insecurities. Is that correct?"

"Yes, that's correct."

"After the defendant was taken into custody, did you attempt to see her?"

"Yes, I only went to the correctional facility that same morning. Officer Davis called to set up the visit."

"And that's the only time you saw her until today, is that correct?"

Not sure what she was getting at, he nervously answered, "Yes, that's correct."

"Mr. Simmons, it seems as though you've become a habitual liar. I heard you mention that same thing to Mr. Bennett in the hall." Turning to the judge she said... "If I have to, Your Honor, I'll swear myself in."

"There's no need, Miss Ortega. You may continue."

"When I went to the correctional facility, I noticed not only your name but a Doctor Berman, a psychiatrist, and the defendant's council's name at least five or six times. Now why are you lying for the defendant? You know you can be held liable for a charge of perjury?"

Joel was beginning to get restless in his chair. He realized he would have to give up more information that he wanted. "Counselor, I realized my wife was having a problem, and for her own safety, I tried to get her help."

"When did you suspect she was having problems severe enough to hire a psychiatrist?"

"Just over a year and a half ago, I thought she was involved in an abusive extramarital affair."

"Why would you think that?"

"She had a few marks on her, like bruises."

"Did you question her about them?"

"Yes, but she never gave me a straight answer."

"Did you ever happen to connect the bruises with, or around the times of your secretaries' disappearances?"

He looked at Veronica with helplessness- a helpless feeling of not having any choice but to give away their secret. "Yes, I was aware of that."

"Objection, Your Honor. The court case at hand is the only thing we should be concerned with."

"On the contrary, Your Honor, it all leads up to a woman possessed with jealousy- enough to eliminate anyone she found a threat to her- whether it was real or imaginary."

"Objection overruled."

"Then you knew positively the defendant- or at least strongly suspected your wife's guilt with the disappearance of the temps?"

"Yes, I did."

"If you will, tell the jury how it began."

"A little more than a year ago, she franticly called my office in the early evening hours. She was crying and very upset."

"Why was she upset?"

"She said the temp I hired brought some cocaine to the shore house. She told me while they were getting high and drinking, the temp died. She didn't know what to do and didn't want to call the authorities."

"Why not?"

"She was afraid there would be an autopsy and feared there would be an investigation after forensics discovered the cocaine in her system."

"So what did you do?"

"I suspected at the time her and Carl Dunn were secretly seeing each other. I told her to call him and tell him what happened, and see what he could do."

"And to your knowledge, did she?"

"Yes, I went down the next morning, it had all been taken care of."

"At that time, did you notice anything unusual about the defendant?"

"Like what, for instance?"

"Any marks or bruises as if she had been involved in a fight?"

"Objection, Your Honor. Council's trying to give the impression if the defendant had any bruises; they were from some sort of physical confrontation with the temp who died. That's not the issue here."

"Objection sustained. Miss Ortega, Please rephrase your question."

"Mr. Simmons, prior to your wife's frantic call telling you about the overdose death of the temp, did you ever observe any physical marks on the defendant?"

"Not that I remember. We weren't seeing that much of each other as husband and wife."

"You mean not sexually where you may have observed any marks?"

"I object Your Honor. Council's still trying to ask the witness things that are of a personal matter. He already stated he couldn't tell because they weren't in each other's company undressed."

"After that incident, did you suspect your wife was involved with the disappearance of any other temps?"

"About three months after that, is when I observed more marks. That's about the same time she really started putting pressure on me about hiring the young secretaries. That's when I hired a private detective to keep tabs on her, Just to make sure she wasn't getting involved in a dangerous relationship."

"Do you suspect she had a part in Karen White's death?"

"I thought she may have, but I didn't really know for sure."

"You told Officer Davis in your interview, she was accusing you of infidelity. Let me just quote your reply to her accusation from his report. You said, addressing the defendant. 'You accusing me of seeing someone else, borders on being hypocritical.' Isn't that what you told him?"

"Yes, that sounds about right."

"You became financial partners with Carl Dunn. Is that correct?"

"Yes, he ran into financial difficulties building my home, and I loaned him some money. Rather than have him owe it to me, he suggested we become partners."

"According to your interview with Officer Davis, You stated he was gambling a lot- and that was the main reason you became partners. Which is true?"

"I guess you could say it was a combination of both. He was stretched pretty far with his ongoing projects. Having a gambling problem didn't help his situation."

"Isn't it true that you allowed the defendant to become the partner to control your interest in his business?"

"Yes."

"If you're marriage was about to end, why did you trust your wife with that responsibility?"

"She seemed very good at it, and it looked like it might help her with the insecurity feeling. I knew by then, her and Carl Dunn, were intimately involved. I thought if she saw how insecure her future was with him financially, she might change her mind and come back with me."

"That wasn't the case, was it?"

"No, it was just the opposite. They became closer together. I felt there was something else that was making the bond between them closer and couldn't imagine what it was."

"Could it be their complicity with another disappearance of a temp?"

"Your Honor, I object. Council is leading the witness."

"Objection sustained. Council will refrain from opinions and stick to facts."

"In your estimation, Mr. Simmons, would it be out of line to acknowledge the defendants' overwhelming desire to control everything surrounding your relationship to the point of assisting Mr. Dunn__...."

"Objection, Your Honor. Council's still trying to create fact out of opinion."

"Objection sustained. Council's been warned. Proceed."

"One more question. In Officers Davis's report, there's a mention of you and Mrs. Simmons having a heated argument in the driveway of your home outside of Philadelphia. Do you remember that?"

"Yes, I do."

"And tell the jury what that fight was about."

"The defendant claimed to have found a set of women's undergarments in the trunk of my car."

"And did the disturbance bring the police?"

"Yes, it seemed as though she wanted to make it loud and embarrassing enough for the neighbor to summon them."

"Did you know the origin of the women's undergarments?"

A muted laugh came from the spectators, as if to say, 'Everyone knows where they originated- they previously adorned some female."

Judge Markert again struck his gavel. "Order..."

"Again, did you know where they came from?"

"No, I never saw them before that minute."

"Was there anything special about them, like being monogrammed?"

"Yes, they had initials on them."

"And do you remember what the initials were?"

"Yes, C.A."

"And did you know what the name of the second temp that went missing was?"

"Yes, Carol Achroth."

"That's right, C.A."

"Does anyone else have access to your auto but you?"

"Only my wife."

"Didn't you connect the initials with the missing temp?"

"I did later, after Karen White was found dead. I thought it was too coincidental not to be connected."

"So you suspected your wife was involved in some way with her disappearance?"

"Yes."

A muted response came from the courtroom.

"No further questions, Your Honor."

"Mr. Denker, would you like to question the witness?"

"No, Your Honor, I would like to recall to the witness stand Officer Davis."

"Officer Davis, Please take the witness stand."

His long strides toward the witness box were with an air of confidence in the testimony he was about to give, and his professional performance of duty.

"Officer, do you realize you're still under oath?"

"Yes Your Honor."

"Then be seated, Mr. Denker. You may proceed."

"Thank you Your Honor. Officer Davis, when you took Mr. Simmons' statement, I take it you did it with his permission."

"Yes, Sir, I made him fully aware of what I was doing."

"In your memory, has he left anything out that may have been damaging to his own credibility?"

"I don't quite know what you mean, counselor, by damaging his own credibility."

"To be more precise, telling the defendant to call Mr. Dunn and see what he could do to help her after the secretary died at the shore house?"

"No, he never mentioned that at all."

"Then why do you suppose he's mentioning it now?"

"I have no idea. Perhaps you should ask him that question."

"Thank you, officer. No further questions, Your Honor."

"You may step down. This court will take a 15 minute recess while council prepares their closing arguments."

Chapter 11

A buzz of quiet conversation went over the room until Judge Markert re-entered.

"Are councils ready?" Looking in their directions, respectively, he said, "Miss Ortega. Mr. Denker?"

They responded in kind... "Yes your honor."

"Mr. Denker, you may proceed."

As Mr. Denker walked over to the jury box to present his case for acquittal, a tense moment spread over the room. Staring directly at the jurors, then in a loud voice he began. "Ladies and Gentleman of the Jury:" The tone of his voice seemed to slice through the tension in the room like a knife, and everyone's eyes were focused on him.

"The case before you that's been presented by the district attorney is based primarily on the scene Mr. Bennett described. A scene we can all agree was horrific to watch but adds up to nothing more than two silhouetted figures- a man strangling a woman. There's no direct connection to the defendant of that scene which took place. Mr. Bennett stated after the body was removed, he saw a shadow of a person- a person he admittedly said- he only saw for a few seconds. From the time he left to alert the authorities, until the time of his return, took over 35 minutes- enough time for the defendant to have possibly not even been there when it took place. She may have just returned home, and was shocked by the scene of the crime. A crime Mr. Dunn admittedly confessed to. With her close relationship with Mr. Dunn and concern for his situation, she had little alternative but to help him. After all, it is her house."

Pausing briefly, he eyed the jury, then continued, "Close your eyes and picture this if you will. You come in your own home to see a friend- a close friend who just killed someone. What do you do? You make a quick decision- an irrational decision in the defendant's case but a decision-none- the less.

Then suddenly there's a knock on the front door. She looks at Carl. 'What should we do? Who do you think that could be?' 'I don't know. I'm not expecting anyone, are you?' 'No. You wait here. I'll answer it.'"

"Opening the door, you see the police. You step back, surprised-that was the look on her face when she opened the door. The look of possibly Carl being arrested for a heinous crime he just committed, not one of 'Oh, I've been caught helping someone who's in serious trouble. Building a case for the defendant's guilt of being a murderer on such facts is pretty farfetched with the testimony presented."

Striding across the room, he stopped in front of Joel. In an almost an accusing gesture, he said "The chloral hydrate bottle described by Mr. Dunn as the one the defendant used to put in the deceased glass, only had her husband's finger prints on it. According to the police, there was no other physical evidence of finger prints on any of the glasses that were used, other than the glasses that were in the dishwasher. It seems to be an attempt to accuse the defendant's husband of destroying the evidence of the deceased. If the defendant's husband prints were on the bottle, he already admitted it may have been when he inadvertently moved it searching the drawer for something. If my client was present, there should have been her prints on one of the glasses on the coffee table and not in the dishwasher, and on the bottle of chloral hydrate also."

The jury began to look at each other, leading me to believe they were contemplating a lack of 100 percent guilt. I thought to myself,

"Could she get off completely scott-free?" I glanced at Veronica. She appeared to be feeling a little more at ease with her council's defense.

"Finally, ladies and gentleman of the jury, having a psychiatrist and a concerned husband visit a troubled woman who's been incarcerated on murder charges shouldn't cast a shadow of guilt on the defendant. To suggest its part of some ongoing treatment of mental instability from obsession with the aging process is purely fictional."

"I move the jury weigh in their final decision what I've just presented. We all come to critical crossroads in life, where the wrong decision can be like a maggot that devours our future. All the evidence against my client comes from a man who's a confessed murderer- an irate husband that was about to ask for a divorce and a person who thought he could become a suitor to my client. A man who claims he was so concerned for her safety, watched as a woman was being strangled to death."

Looking most solemnly at each juror, Mr. Denker said, "I urge you to keep these things in perspective while you're rendering your decision." After a long pause, he said, "Thank You!"

Judge Markert announced, "Miss Ortega, you may address the jury."

"Thank you, Your Honor. Ladies and Gentleman of the jury, you've heard the plea of innocents for the defendant from Mr. Denker. If it wasn't for knowing how the defense is trying to distance the defendant from being an accomplice to Heather O'Brien's murder. I could see where she could have easily been chosen as a candidate for sainthood. The defense fails to note that Mr. Simmons testified he specifically saw bruises around the defendant's neck, and upper body on several occasions over the past year. In fact, he was so concerned he hired a private detective to follow her. He also testified, he observed them around the same time of his different secretary's disappearances.

He further testified that he thought, and I quote, 'I thought there was a strong possibility Veronica had something to do with their disappearances.' I might further add__" Holding up the picture taken of the defendant when she arrived at the detention center. "These pictures clearly show she had fresh bruises around her neck and upper body." passing them to the jury once again for their review.

"If you compare them with the marks on the neck of Heather O'Brien, take note, ladies and gentleman of the jury, they look the same. It appears they were most likely locked in an intense struggle, strangling each other. The deceased being a much bigger girl, was probably over-powering the defendant to a point where Carl Dunn had to come to her rescue. That's when he must have struck the deceased on the side of the head, then finish strangling her." Miss Ortega turned, pointing at Veronica in a stern accusing voice. "A task the defendant who's sitting there began- and stood silently witnessing it."

Scanning the jury she continued... "Ask yourself this question. If you knew you were less physically capable of killing a person, espe-cially by strangling them, what would you have to do, to compensate the unequal strength?" Looking at the jury- individually, eyeing each one as if she was waiting for a response, she loudly proclaimed. "You would have to have an equalizer. And what better way to do that than to offer the person a drink- a drink laced with chloral hydrate in it. A drink that wasn't potent enough to make the desired effect on Heather O'Brien right away, but only made her aware there was something wrong- defi-nitely wrong- terribly wrong. She must have struggled to her feet, des-perately trying to get to the front door- a door that represented safety, a door that was her only hope of getting away from the defendant and her murderess intention, only to have her path to that safety blocked-blocked by the defendant herself- the defendant who sealed her hor-rible fate. The defendant who didn't just come in while Mr. Bennett was getting the police, as the defense is trying to make you believe."

Miss Ortega, driving her point home, approached the juror's box, and with her small fist, pounded on the rail. Like a blacksmith would pound out a piece of hot metal with a rhythm, she raised her voice con-tinuing with her accusations.

"She had- to have- been there- all along. To further cement her part of the evening, according to Officer Davis's testimony, Mr. Dunn's car had to have been parked within walking distance of where the body was dumped. That, ladies and gentleman, puts the final touches on this case- a case for pre-meditated murder.

"Carl Dunn may have been the physical murderer, but the defendant is equally guilty, luring the victim to the shore house to kill her. And that ladies and gentlemen, makes her just as guilty in the eyes of the law. When you retire to discuss the innocence or guilt of the defendant__" Pointing to Veronica again. "Think about the real Mrs. Simmons. Not the Mrs. Simmons you see sitting before you. The one who led Mr. Bennett to believe her own husband was possibly a serial killer. Now ask yourself one more question, for what reason?"

A silence that was deafening was felt, as everyone anticipating Miss Ortega's answer.

In a loud voice: "I'll tell you that reason. She was setting up Mr. Bennett as a witness. A witness to her defense of her personal fiction that her husband was so abusive, he was responsible for the marks on her neck. The mentally abusive husband who always wanted to know where she was and what she was doing. The husband who was so terrible- in truth- gave her the lavish lifestyle she wanted. Was there another reason she wanted Mr. Bennett to believe her husband was guilty? Was it some sort of elaborate scheme, so the blame for the murdered victims- the victims that her husband employed- could rest squarely on Mr. Simmons' shoulders?"

Leaning on the separation panel of the jury box once more, sternly eyeing each juror again she concluded… "That ladies and gentleman of the jury, is something we'll never know."

Miss Ortega's closing argument seemed to have ignited another spark with the jury, and I think Veronica sensed it. She began to get restless in her chair.

Judge Markert remarked, "Are there any other questions?"

Without a response from either council, he continued. "Will the court officer please conduct the jury to the juror's room to contemplate their decision."

Court bailiff announced, "All rise as the judge retires to his private chambers."

After the judge and jury left, Veronica, after some discussion with her attorney, was ushered out of the room. Silence was broken by the conversations of the remaining spectators discussing the case as they exited the court room.

I asked… "Miss Ortega, in your professional opinion, how does this case look?"

I could see her hesitance to reply with Joel still sitting there and again motioned to me by nodding her head to join her outside the courtroom.

"Ron, I'd rather you not discuss this in front of Joel. This case isn't over yet. It should be obvious he's helping her defense council. Someone wiped those prints off that bottle, and it could only be one person- Joel."

"I guess it doesn't look to good for Carl Dunn, does it?"

"Not at all: I'm hoping she gets a life sentence out of this, but right now I can't see how that's going to happen. Even if it does- her attorney will certainly ask for an appeal. We'll just have to wait and see."

"Do you think the jury will take long with the deliberation?"

"I don't know. The longer they're retired, the more they're debating the different points of testimony. That never bodes well for the prosecution.

Laughing lightly she continued. "Her defense attorney really poked holes in the case. He made you look like someone that was preying on an innocent helpless woman."

"Yea, it wasn't my most comfortable feeling as a witness. I would have bought tickets to a stage play with this much drama. Are you hanging around the court room hoping for a quick decision from the jury?"

"No, I have to go back to the district attorney's office. I have some more paperwork to finish… how about you?"

"I might just as well go back to the police station with Ben and wait there. He let me use his typewriter before. Maybe I can get this story started while I'm waiting. I don't want to drive all the way back to the city. Could you give me a call there when it's time to have the verdict read?"

"No problem. I think Officer Davis wants to be here to listen too."

Going back to the car, I couldn't help but try to understand why Joel was still defending her. He seemed sincere the night it happened when I tried to apologize for causing him grief. He had me convinced that I was a life saver. He actually thanked me. Why the change?

Getting back to the police station, I knocked- then entered the room.

"Ben, do you mind if I lean on you for a couple of favors?"

"As long as you don't lean too hard... What is it?"

"First, I'd like to call my neighbor and have her take care of Daisy's constitutional. Second, I'd like to borrow the typewriter to begin my story for the paper."

Kevin was in the room putting on his coat, getting ready to go out on patrol remarked, while laughing, "The phone call and typewriter are free. The paper is where we make all our money for the coffee fund."

It brought a laugh from Ben as he waved his hand at Kevin. "Don't listen to Kevin. We're running a special today- fifty cents a sheet."

I laughed. "Don't worry- this story will make the paper a lot of money on increased circulation. Quite a few people have been following this case. I'll make sure they shuffle some appreciation in your direction."

"That's not necessary. We were only kidding. The paper is in the top cabinet right over the desk."

"Thanks, Ben__"

I began to get into the meat of my story, when I suddenly thought of something. "Ben, I think we can agree that Joel went to the house first before coming here."

Ben swiveled around in his chair. "What do you mean?"

Veronica always suggested he's a clean freak, but when I went to his apartment, I noticed he's even a bigger slob than me. It makes me laugh that the opposite applies. He's such a slob. He forgot to turn on the dishwasher."

"Hey, that's right!" He laughed, "That's one time the lie backfired."

Just then the phone rang and Ben answered it. It was Miss Ortega... "The jury has reached a verdict- they'll be ready to announce it in a half hour."

I thought she was right- a quick decision sounded positive. It's only been an hour and a half. We got in the car and headed for the court room.

It was almost 6:30 and only a few spectators returned to the court-room. After everyone was seated, the jury was ushered into the room. Veronica, escorted by a prison matron took her seat next to her defense lawyer.

"All rise as Judge Markert enters the room."

After taking his seat, he looked at the jurors, then asked, "Ladies and gentleman of the jury, have you reached a verdict?"

The jury foreman rose from his chair. "Yes, we have, Your Honor."

"Will the defendant please rise and face the jury_."

A sudden quietness enveloped the room... Quietness so still, the ticking of the large clock on the wall in the back of the room could be easily heard. The moment was intense as everyone held their breath.

"Your Honor, we find the defendant, Veronica Simmons, guilty as charged."

The tenseness suddenly disappeared with those words, and I felt comfortable that justice had temporarily been served. I glanced at Veronica, trying to see any sign of remorse. There was none- a blank stare as though her whole world just came crashing down around her, and in essence, it had.

The courtroom was abuzz with conversation until Judge Markert banged his gavel.

"Mrs. Veronica Simmons, this jury has found you guilty as charged. Is there anything you would like to say in your defense?"

Looking to her lawyer seemingly for advice, with a nod from him replied, "No your honor!"

"If the defense wishes to petition the court for an appeal, he has 15 days in which to comply."

Looking at his calendar... Judge Markert glanced up.

"If no appeal is forthcoming, Veronica Simmons, you'll be sentenced on the 17th of February of this year at 2:30 PM: in this courtroom."

Turning to the jury the judge said, "Ladies and gentleman of the jury, thank you for your service and candidness in rendering your decision. This jury is dismissed. This case is closed."

The court baillif announced... "All rise while the judge leaves the room."

With Judge Markert retiring to his chamber, the remaining spectators began filing out of the courtroom, some still quietly debating the jury's verdict.

I turned to Miss Ortega. "Well, when you said she might have gotten away with it I was disappointed, I'm glad you were wrong. Do you think her attorney will file an appeal?"

Gathering her files and returning them to her briefcase, she replied, "I don't know?" She briefly paused. "He may just weigh the summary I gave in my closing remarks and think it might be better- to just throw herself on the mercy of the judge- that's a hard call."

Ben remarked, "I've heard some closing arguments before, but I have to say, yours has to be the most memorable."

"Ben, I agree. It was very impressive. I won't be able to capture that moment in the article I have to write. I think what did it was the banging on the jurors box with a closed fist. It put the fear of god in them. They were too afraid to find her not guilty."

They all laughed... "Careful, you two will give me a big head. I haven't been in this game very long."

Ben and I looked at each other. "Well, if you're new at this, you sure could have fooled the hell out of us." I said.

She asked, "Ron, if there is an appeal, I'll let you know. It's been a pleasure dealing with you again, Officer Davis, you too." Then she reached out and shook both our hands.

Looking to the back of the courtroom, I saw Joel in conversation with Veronica's lawyer. Mr. Denker seemed to be shaking his head no at whatever Joel was asking.

"Miss Ortega, I wonder what that conversation's all about?" I drew her attention to them. "Do you think he's asking the lawyer to forget an appeal because it might come back at him covering for her?"

She glanced up. "Possibly, I think I impressed on him he was liable for a few counts of perjury and obstruction of justice. Telling his wife to call Carl Dunn and have him dispose of the body puts him right in the mix. He may still love his wife, but I don't think he wants to trade places with her."

Ben asked, "Are you ready to leave Ron? I have to get back to the station."

"Yes, I still have a story to complete before the deadline at midnight."

As we approached Joel and Veronica's attorney standing at the back of the room, they stopped talking. I nodded at Joel as I went by, and he nodded back in return. Before we were out the door, they resumed talking. I looked at Ben. I think Miss Ortega was right. There won't be an appeal.

We drove back to the police station, and I walked inside with Ben.

Kevin, seeing us come in, remarked, "Ben, The mayor was here a little while ago with another member of town council. They couldn't express their gratitude enough."

Ben jokingly replied, "Did you mention a raise might be a nice way to express it?"

"He told me to let you know he'll stop by tomorrow. I think they want to give us some kind of award."

I commented, "Well, guys, I have to get back to Philly and write this story."

Kevin jokingly said, "The correct spelling is, *OFFICER KEVIN JONES* and *OFFICER BEN DAVIS* for the record…

Kevin had the wit of someone perfect for the job- someone who could find some humor in almost any situation. Ben too!

Walking out the door, I remarked, "I won't misspell your names. I wouldn't want to get back to my car and find a parking ticket."

I had the story laid out in my mind of how I was going to write it. Since the plea came in as guilty, I didn't have to worry about writing the story the way I wanted. I was going to label Veronica for the conniver she really was.

Realizing what a narrow escape I had, almost getting wrapped up in a situation like that- was a relief in itself. No more worries about Veronica. No more worries about her make-believe world. No more worries about wondering whether anyone was following me.

Like a giant Millstone lifted off my back, I felt liberated. In the spring when the fish begin to return again, I can go back to my favorite spot clear of mind. I may stop in and see Ben and Kevin. After all, they were the ones who put out the light to this bad dream.

Sitting back I thought to myself, "What would I feel the next time I see Veronica's house?" Pity... I can't think of anything else. Pity, that's it.

My mind shifted to the neighbor who was supposed to look in on Daisy. Daisy- boy I have a lot of lost time with her to make up for. You know, Ben told me he had a Black Lab. I'll have to stop and see him again.

Something else- The neighbor who looks in on Daisy, it's really thoughtful. She's been a tenant for the last year. We've had a few good conversations. Maybe I can thank her by taking her out to dinner? I'll have to put that on my list of things to do...

The End